Twelve of

Ten true tales and two that could be

Anthony Holt

ISBN: 978-1-326-24213-8

Anthony Holt MBE was a pilot and seaman officer in the Royal Navy for over thirty years, after which he began a second career running two of London's larger 'Gentlemen's Clubs' for the next eighteen years.

He is married and lives in Dorset where he now spends his time writing, sailing and working as a volunteer Coast Watcher.

Disclosure

'One Soldier's Story' was related to me by my father and it is an unusual account of how he was one of the last soldiers to leave the Dunkirk beaches. I have no reason to doubt its veracity because when I first heard the story the details were presented precisely, calmly and objectively. When the British Expeditionary Force was collapsing and in retreat there were, no doubt, many stories of a breakdown in discipline and this is but one. Conversely, there are many more accounts of individual heroism, which may well have been lost in the sands of Dunkirk.

The details are accurate but some of the names of individuals and military units have been changed . The name of the little ship *Bullfinch* has not been changed. The ship and her civilian crew deserve to be remembered for what they achieved in 1940.

'Adventure in Lyme Bay' is an amalgamation of two events which took place in the waters off the Dorset coast. In one, the yacht was very nearly overwhelmed in a vicious summer storm. In the other, the group of three dolphins arrived from nowhere to play with the boat, directing it, controlling its heading, lying close alongside and finally giving a dramatic display of leaping and turning centred entirely on the boat.

'The Flight' is entirely a work of fiction and is daring to suggest how things might have been for one of the early pioneers of aviation.

'The Voyage' is a work of fiction and fantasy, suggesting perhaps how things might be in time to come.

'A Walk in the Desert' is another of the many stories of the Second World War told to me by my father. It relates a curious event set after the Battle of El Alamein, when the Afrika Corps was collapsing in the face of the British onslaught. I believe the events described are accurate in every detail.

'The Political Interview' describes the extraordinary and incompetent arrangements set in place to go through the motions of selecting a candidate to stand for office while actually, and privately, having already made the decision.

'The King of Spain's Father' is the rather bizarre story of the high level decision to promote Don Juan Carlos, the father of King Juan Carlos of Spain, from the honorary rank of Lieutenant in the Royal Navy, to the honorary rank of Admiral in the Royal Navy – and of course the implementation of that decision for which the Author was made responsible. It was a sequence of events that were encapsulated in possible disaster and diplomatic embarrassment throughout.

'The Secretary From Hell'. Every Employer will know that despite the most careful recruitment process, the successful candidate does not always match the glowing reports received at and before the interviews.

In 'The Garden Party'. The Author was responsible for the distribution, to worthy applicants, of five hundred invitations to Her Majesty's Royal Garden Parties each year. This was never an easy task, but it was sometimes amusing.

'Trooping the Colour'. Here the Author was desperately trying to prevent a senior admiral from making a fool of himself on a very important national occasion.

'A Visit to the Seychelles' describes two incidents which took place during an official visit by a British cruiser to the Seychelles Islands. The first incident demonstrates just how far some will go to create political or diplomatic embarrassment and the second shows how wind and waves can so easily combine to destroy the most careful of plans.

'Fire on the Road' is the story of how the Author suddenly found himself in a life or death crises while driving home for the weekend.

The characters presented in these stories are not meant to represent any individuals, alive or deceased.

Acknowledgements

Again I am grateful for the humour, guidance, patience and general support of my wife, which enables me to immerse myself in my writing, and for my father, the author of two of these tales.

My thanks to Brian Johnstone MBE, who located and allowed me to use the image of the Luscombe 8E Silvaire Delux VR-BAK float plane which is depicted on the front cover.

Dedication

This book is dedicated to my family.

Contents

A Visit to the Seychelles

Fire on the Road

One Soldier's Story

It was the middle of May and we had been in France for several months with nothing much happening. Most of our heavy vehicles had been driven down to Southampton and then onto several elderly tank-landing ships for the journey along the south coast and across the Channel to Dieppe where they had been driven back down the ramps to wait for the rest of the company. The remainder of the wagons destined for France had been craned onto the decks of a couple of freighters in Dover to be offloaded a few hours later in Calais, from where they headed south to join up with the group coming from Dieppe at a rendezvous just to the west of Arras, where our Royal Army Service Corps unit had been ordered to assemble, prior to running supplies up to the forward units of the British Expeditionary Force. Most of the lorries and vans that formed the Company had been hastily requisitioned from their civilian owners and the names of butchers, grocers and bakers still showed through the thin khaki camouflage paint. We were, truly, a motley lot.

We had been carrying supplies for the 4th British Division as they advanced into Belgium and we were now heading back towards the coast to reload with food and ammunition. The roads had begun to clog up with refugees trying to escape the advancing German Panzer Divisions and progress was slow. A few miles outside Ghent, the CO decided that our unit should pull off the road into a grass meadow and bivouac for the night. He called the officers and senior NCOs together to explain that we would make better progress in the early morning, so everybody should be ready to leave one hour after first light.

1

The trucks were scattered around the sloping field of lush grass and the men bedded down in small groups well clear of the vehicles. I took my bedroll and, with my friend Sid Vickers, who was also a sergeant, settled down on the far side of the field where the ground began to slope upward again.

I was in the deep sleep of exhaustion when I was shattered into wakefulness by several things happening at once. The air seemed filled with a mind-stopping, roaring noise, accompanied by a rushing wind. At the same time the ground immediately to my right was exploding in a series of eruptions, as though some giant seamstress was applying a line of stitching across the turf. Sid was also awake and shouting something which I could not hear, but I could see the cause of the drama. My gaze was riveted on a big black cross decorating the underside of the wing of the aircraft that had just attempted to kill us. As I watched it disappear, skimming low over the field, I thought that the fighter or whatever it was must surely hit the rising ground in front of it. But it didn't, and suddenly it was gone, leaving just ringing ears and shock in its wake.

Each of us stood for a moment staring at the rows of exploded holes in the turf, made by the aircraft's cannon and machine guns, neatly framing the spot where we had chosen to sleep. The pilot had flown so low in his vain attempt to kill us that we had been inside the cone of his fire, the focal point of which would have been some distance into the ground beneath us. Curiously, few of the vehicles scattered about the field behind us seemed to have been damaged.

Other men were milling around in the shadowy pre-dawn light so, picking up our kit, we trudged back across the field towards the wagons, two of which had actually been hit, and were riddled by cannon fire. I thought we should be preparing

2

to move out but nothing seemed to be happening. Then I realised that there were no officers. With Sid, I carried out a quick search of our temporary camp; but we couldn't find the CO or any other officers. They had gone and so had their cars, four of them. Sid suggested that they might have gone to look for orders but even as he said it he realised that could not be the case with all of them. They had run away.

I was the senior sergeant of the unit so I thought I had better do something to get the men moving, or at least find someone who could tell us what we were required to do. The road alongside our field was already beginning to fill up with trucks, carts, people on foot and animals – as well as small groups of British military vehicles, all heading west. We had two motorbikes for despatch riders so I took one of them to try to find out what we should do. I had little doubt that for the time being, we had seen the last of our officers, who were an unimpressive collection of 'hostilities only' people led by an elderly self-serving major who had never before seen action, despite the stories he liked to tell.

I had barely reached the road before I was stopped by a sergeant of the Military Police. He looked strangely out of place with his crisp, smart red cap, but he was brief and brutal in his instruction.

"You can see what's happening," he said. "We are in a general retreat towards the coast at Dunkirk and Jerry isn't far behind. Burn your vehicles and destroy your equipment, then get on the road."

"On foot?" I asked, with all the shock of he who is used to driving everywhere.

"Yes, on bloody foot!" he shouted over the rising din of the retreating column of humanity. "You won't get trucks through this lot and orders are to deny everything to the enemy. On

3

foot! Got that?" He turned away and slotted himself back into the passenger seat of his strange little open top French car as his driver moved purposefully into the crowd.

I had indeed 'got that'. But I didn't think I wanted to 'get that'; and in the few minutes that it took to get the bike back along the road and into the field I had formed the view that with the British Army evidently in full retreat it was 'every man for himself' – a conclusion our six officers had reached earlier that morning.

As I reappeared, bumping down across the grass to where the men were gathering together, I was formulating a plan.

"The whole bloody army is heading for the beach," I said.

"Christ help us!" someone said.

"That's where the bloody 'Ruperts' went," came another voice.

"Okay. The redcaps have told us to wreck and burn all our vehicles, take personal weapons and packs and join the road for Dunkirk, but since nobody is around to check up on us I've got a better idea." There was a general murmur which could have been support or mutiny; but it was silenced by Sid.

"Shaddup and listen!" he shouted. The men quietened and waited for me to continue, but I could see a lot of truculent expressions. Discipline was dying on the vine.

I pressed on. "We need to get out of here but quick, so we take the six best and smallest trucks and head for Dunkirk," I said. Although not all of my listeners knew where Dunkirk was, I realised I had got their attention. "Everything else we burn." This seemed to produce action. Men swarmed back to the lorries and vans, darting in and out to retrieve possessions and weapons. Within fifteen minutes six of the smaller trucks were lined up at the entrance to the field which was now covered in thick black smoke, punctured by yellow flames

4

streaming low across the meadows on the westerly wind. Each small lorry was fitted with a Bren gun mounted on the roof of the cab and could carry six or seven men in addition to the driver and gunner. A gnarled old former Great War corporal and two men from the last lorry stood across the road with their rifles and barred the flow of refugees long enough to allow the six small canvas-covered lorries to trundle out onto the road in tight convoy.

As we drove west the refugee stream eased and most of the military vehicles we passed were smashed up or burning wrecks. The army was in full retreat. From time to time we saw a single enemy aircraft flying low over the roads. Occasionally a bomb would be dropped or, more likely, they would fire machine guns at chance military or civilian targets – including us. As soon as an aircraft was seen we tried to get off the road, attempting to hide among the trees that lined most of this route. It was on one of these stops that Sid, who had elected to be my gunner in the lead vehicle, stood up on his seat with his head and shoulders through the hatch and fired off a sustained burst at a Jerry plane foolishly flying low and fairly slowly along the road. As the aircraft passed over the top of the truck it was trailing thick brown smoke and only seconds later it exploded as it hit the trees a hundred yards to the right of us.

A vast pall of smoke across the whole of our front from left to right accompanied by devastation on every side indicated that we were approaching the town of Dunkirk. The civilian refugees seemed to have melted away, perhaps in the hope of finding sanctuary further to the south; and the roads were packed with military so that nobody took any notice of our small convoy.

Buildings seemed to be burning on all sides as our lorries threaded their way through the north-eastern outskirts of the town. Progress became even slower as we struggled around fallen masonry and wrecked vehicles. We were approaching the northern beaches but first had to negotiate a bridge over a wide canal. I stopped the truck two hundred yards short of the bridge and hopped out to have a look ahead on foot. The bridge was approached around a bend in the road and I could see that it was manned by a small group of Belgian soldiers who had set up a barricade and were turning away all vehicles that approached them.

I trotted back to the truck and then beyond it down the line of the other five, shouting brief instructions to each driver. I told them we would run the bridge and break through the barrier. I would lead and all they had to do was keep close up.

We rolled slowly forward, gently gathering pace, until the bridge guards became aware of the convoy bearing down on them. The Belgian soldiers stood on either side of the makeshift barrier and levelled their rifles at my truck. I made myself as small as I could and rammed the throttle to the floor. The six trucks charged forward and my windscreen was shattered by a bullet as we smashed through the barrier. A small gap had opened up and the driver of the second truck lost his nerve. With bullets pinging off the front of his cab he squealed to a stop causing the other four behind to stop as well. Through what remained of my mirror, I could see our soldiers climbing out with hands held high.

There was nothing to be done so I accelerated away. Eight miles later we arrived at the beaches at a place called Bray Dunes. A few hundred yards short of the beach we found a big detached house, half of which had been destroyed. With a bit of lifting and shifting of rubble we managed to back the lorry

6

into what had once been a drawing room and then put a reasonable camouflage of rubble and rubbish around it. If all else failed, there was the faint possibility of a ride out of the beach redoubt.

We tramped the three hundred or so yards down to the dunes and, with Sid and the other half dozen men who had ridden with me, I began to search for our officers. After about an hour we located them sitting in a disconsolate group waiting for the chance to get off the beach, and looking distinctly sheepish when the small squad of two sergeants and six soldiers marched up to them.

The Major concocted some cock and bull story about being summoned to 'Headquarters' – wherever that might have been – and then becoming cut off, before travelling in the same direction as the rest of the army, sure in the knowledge that we would catch up. He didn't explain the need for all his officers to travel with him, nor their combined ability to reach the beach at Dunkirk. I wondered where their cars were.

The Major sat on his little hillock of sand and asked where the rest of the NCOs and men were. I replied that they were on foot and would probably arrive within a few hours; and since the interview then seemed to be over, I went to sit under a nearby grass-topped dune. Despite the noise I dozed until prodded awake by Sid. Our people were walking towards us in a column along the beach. They still seemed in pretty good order as they stopped on the sand in front of our now silent and useless Major.

A young lieutenant re-joined the group, having been sent reconnoitring further along the beach towards the harbour. After a short conversation with the Major he strolled across to where I sat, surrounded by the troops, and told me that our

Company was to follow 21 Company to be lifted off in Navy boats.

While standing on the sand in front of the Major I asked if anyone knew where 21 Company was to be found. Glances were exchanged and shoulders shrugged. Nobody knew, or cared it seemed. I suggested that perhaps someone should go and find them.

"Do you think anyone would go and look for them?" asked the Major, uncertainly.

"I've got nothing better to do," I said. "I'll go and look for them myself." There was no answer so I saluted the wreck of a man in front of me, turned as smartly as I could on the soft sand and strode away. Before I had gone ten yards, my friend Sid joined me and together we strode off down the beach in the late afternoon sunshine, which contrasted with the towering columns of smoke and flames from the town beyond the dunes.

Within just over an hour we found 21 Company and I reported to the Captain, who was now the Company Commander and very much in charge of his situation – quite unlike our own Commander.

He told me that his Company was to be lifted off the beach at 0300 and that he thought our Company would be able to follow his off the beach. Sid stayed with 21 Company and joined them in digging holes in the sand while I went back along the beach and reported what we had found.

The Major, who had brightened up a bit by now, told me to go back and wait with 21 Company until their embarkation was under way and then to report back to fetch our troops. I set off back to 21 Company.

At about 0300 hours several Navy boats came into the shallows and our new comrades started wading out to climb aboard. There was little for Sid and me to do so we both went

8

off along the harder sand at the waterline to fetch our own Company. Twenty minutes later we reached the empty spot where they had been. They had gone, leaving nothing but bits of rubbish and indentations in the sand. We turned and headed back the way we had come only to find, after a further twenty minutes, that 21 Company had also gone.

Thoroughly depressed now, we made our way back up the beach and lay down at the edge of the dunes. I slept for a couple of hours but was woken by the intermittent thud of a gun, not far away. Sid, who was already awake, pointed; and in the thin morning light I could see a single Bofors gun manned by one gunner who was shooting ineffectually at occasional aircraft which I assumed to be German.

"At least he's still fighting," said Sid quietly. I looked beyond the gunner towards the burning town where it was evident that the battle was still raging and the rear-guard was holding out. In front of us the beach seemed to have largely emptied, with far fewer groups of men near the water's edge, a few lone stragglers wandering or sitting about and some unburied bodies lying on the sand where they had fallen. Out to sea there was nothing.

We decided to go in search of food and water and as we walked along the beach we began to be joined by other soldiers who had lost their units. Most of these seemed to be RASC or Royal Engineers. By about midday our little band of stragglers had risen to nineteen men. We had located a small amount of water which we shared out, but no food. We also saw that a couple of warships had appeared a mile or so off the beach and four boats were coming in towards a group of men assembling at the water's edge.

This was another mixture of strays, organised and controlled by a Royal Engineer Captain and a Regimental Sergeant Major, both of whom had drawn revolvers and were threatening to shoot any man who misbehaved. I approached the Captain and he agreed that we could attach our men to the end of the queue providing that Sid and I took over control when they left with their men.

When the last of the Royal Engineers group left, we were given the revolvers and the boats kept coming in, taking sixteen of our men out to the ships, leaving just three of us – Sid, me and a tough little Liverpudlian corporal called Dutchy Holland. We moved back out of the shallows and waited; but none of the boats came back. We had been abandoned.

It was once more late in the afternoon and, not fancying another hungry, miserable night on the beach, the three of us went off to look for more substantial shelter.

We foraged among abandoned packs and equipment which produced some food, mostly dry biscuits, but also several canteens with fresh water. By the late twilight we had spotted a derelict house – or at least the lower half of a house. It seemed to be deserted and stood silhouetted against the smoky, oily flames still pouring from the town. It wasn't much but at least it might provide shelter; so the three of us felt our way in through a shattered door and down some steps into a basement. There was no light at all in the room but there seemed to be other people sleeping there so we flopped down among them and fell immediately into the sleep of exhaustion.

"Sarge, we gotta get outa here." Dutchy was vigorously shaking my shoulder and as I opened my eyes the first thing I saw was his face, inches from mine, with an unmistakable look of horror on it. I moved my head and through the dim morning light I could see that the room was full of French, Belgian and British soldiers – all of them dead. Sid stirred as I clambered up and at the same time noticed the stench of death. We had spent the night in a makeshift morgue.

We wasted no time in getting out of there. Inevitably we headed back towards the beach, which now seemed to be pretty well deserted. The tide was out and, seemingly far away, sat an ancient, scruffy, steam powered coaster. It was heavily loaded with troops and sat, aground, in about two feet of water. We debated whether we should attempt to get on board but there didn't seem much point because the ship must have come in empty on a rising tide and was now heavily loaded and stuck fast. She didn't seem likely to be going anywhere soon. We sat on the sand and watched as the tide came in steadily on the slightly shelving beach, and the water level rose correspondingly slowly up the side of the ship.

"*Bullfinch*," said Sid.

"What?"

"*Bullfinch* – that's the old tub's name. You can see it on the wheelhouse."

I looked at the ship and noticed that some of the occupants were waving to us – signalling us to join them. We wondered whether to try but I was dubious. "The only way that ship is going to get off this beach is when the Jerry artillery blows it off," I said gloomily. My companions continued to discuss the likely fate of the ship while I was distracted by the fact that the noise of battle from the town behind us seemed to have died away.

"We should give it a go," said Sid, already on his feet. "We've got nothing here except a Jerry bullet or a prison camp."

I stood up and looked across the expanse of sea between us and the ship, which now seemed to be sitting in about five feet of water but still solidly aground.

Two merchant seamen were now waving and shouting to us from the bows of the old coaster and another was waving urgently from the wheelhouse. I heard the words "last chance" and the others must have heard it too. Without further comment, we three abandoned soldiers waded into the water towards the ship. As the depth increased to waist height, the pull of the water on our thick, soaked battledress made our progress seem like trying to wade through glue. My gaze was riveted on the name *Bullfinch* now growing steadily bigger in front of me and I pondered how this, which only minutes before we had been content to ignore, had now become a vital goal.

The water was chest high but we still had several yards to go and I could see the anxious faces of the crew encouraging our progress, as well as the faces of the soldiers crowding the deck, mostly devoid of expression. Sid was taller than me and he was a yard or so ahead when a wire and rope ladder was lowered from the deck. It reached only to about a foot above the water line but Sid lunged forward with one clutching arm raised and his face in the water. I attempted another step but there was nothing there and I tumbled forward, disappearing momentarily before a hand grabbed at the immersed collar of my battledress and heaved upward. As my head came clear I saw a second ladder with a man clinging to it with one hand while his other hand was fastened on to me. Other hands appeared as well as some ropes; and with adrenalin pumping, we were dragged soggily up towards the bulwark lining the ship's side and over it to collapse at the feet of the other bewildered and traumatised passengers.

The tide continued to roll in and the water climbed up the rusty side of the ancient steamer but she remained stuck fast. The man in the wheelhouse peered out of the window from under a greasy flat cap and said something to a crewman on deck. The ship began to vibrate and rumble as the engine was started. *Bullfinch* didn't move despite at least two more attempts lasting nearly an hour to drive the ship off the sand with the engine. Somebody said that it was now high tide and I began to give up the hope that had been briefly raised.

The skipper poked his head out of the wheelhouse once more and spoke again to the two crewmen on deck. One of them went below while the other one came aft and climbed up on to a hatch cover. He ordered everyone up on to their feet and as the weary soldiery began to obey him, he explained that we were all to move over to one side of the ship, then back as quickly as we could to the other side, to try to dislodge the ship by causing it to rock.

We were desperate to get away; and all of the men who could followed the instruction and went over to the right hand side of the ship, then at a signal from the crewman we all shambled and ran to the other side then back again, by which time the engine was running again and the vibration was back. We kept this up for about three or four minutes until at last the *Bullfinch* seemed to jerk, then rock of her own accord, then glide smoothly off the sand into deeper water.

Our troubles were not yet over. Within half an hour of leaving the beach the previously empty sky began to fill with aircraft. Fighters were circling each other at high level; but it was a group of Stukas which took our attention. They came over at medium level in formation and peeled off one at a time, diving almost vertically with an accompanying scream and each aiming two bombs at us before pulling out of the dive. The scruffy old skipper peered up at the attacking aircraft and as each set of bombs was released he turned the ship through ninety degrees, so the bombs fell on either side rather than on

13

the bows and stern. The second wave of Stukas seemed wise to this and adjusted their aim but the old man outwitted them every time, sometimes going hard astern or turning and charging towards the diving aircraft to get behind it.

This contest continued as *Bullfinch* struggled on across the Channel. Eventually, with the afternoon light fading, the Stukas gave up; but by this time *Bullfinch* was disabled, with the engine, propeller shaft and steering all damaged by the dozens of 'near miss' bombs. In fact, the last of a pair of Stukas was shot down by a small corvette which arrived from the direction of Dover, and to unheard cheers from the men on deck, his companion failed to pull out of his dive while trying to realign his aim.

Astern of the corvette, a big tug bustled up; and two hours later *Bullfinch* was towed into Ramsgate Harbour. Red Cross people, troops and officials crowded round as those of us who could walk held up our heads and marched off the ship as best we could – which probably wasn't very impressive. We were put on a train to Chester, given tea, cakes, cigarettes, and sandwiches at every stop, while some slept, some wept, and many just sat and gave silent thanks for their deliverance.

Adventure in Lyme Bay

"Let go for'ard!" I called, and on cue Jenny deftly slipped the bow rope and flicked it back onto the deck at her feet. At the same time I eased the throttle gently into astern and the boat moved slowly back along the 'finger' pontoon. I held on to the stern rope, keeping tension on it to hold the stern close to the pontoon as the boat slid backward and started to turn out of the berth. At the last moment I threw the wheel hard over to port and the thirty-three foot boat continued to back gracefully out of her berth and then to move astern down between the lines of moored boats.

The morning was perfect. Although still early, the air was warm with a slight breeze from the south-east and the sky a clear blue from horizon to horizon. We stooged around in front of the lifting bridge with half a dozen other yachts and two big white motor cruisers, nodding greetings and waiting for eight o'clock. The church clock began to chime, a face peered over the bridge parapet by the control cabin, the three green 'traffic lights' came on and the barriers dropped across the road. A booming voice announced to lingering pedestrians that the bridge was about to be raised and after thirty seconds the sections began to move upward. The waiting vessels had jockeyed themselves into position and since we were in no particular hurry I had found and held a place near the end of the queue.

We each waved to the bridge operator in his cabin as we motored past the raised bridge arms, receiving a nod in return. The dog was sitting up on a cockpit seat to get a better view of the world passing by and we were on our way. Jenny was

15

already collecting and stowing the fenders ready for the open sea and I concentrated on keeping clear of the variety of waterborne traffic that was buzzing about in the outer harbour, all taking advantage of a beautiful early June morning.

As we cleared the harbour entrance I turned the yacht into the south-easterly breeze to hoist sails, a manoeuvre which for once went perfectly; and within three or four minutes we were motor-sailing at a mile-eating seven knots towards Portland Bill. Although my passage plan had been set for a route around the outside of the notorious Portland Race, I could see that conditions to the south of the 'Bill' were so benign that it should be easy to slip round close-in through the inshore passage. This would save several miles and reduce our passage time to Torquay by perhaps an hour. There were two boats ahead of us, both apparently heading for the inner passage, so when we were settled 'in the groove' behind them, I flicked on the auto-pilot and pulled a folded piece of paper from my pocket. The faxed inshore weather report for sea area Portland suggested a typical summer day. We were in the lower edge of a fading anti-cyclone which was providing the south-easterly breeze, but otherwise there was not likely to be much activity. I did look carefully at what seemed to be the forecaster's afterthought, written right at the end of the report. "Slight possibility of a weak thundery trough moving from Northern France into the Western Channel later in the period," it said. I looked up at the perfect day around me, folded the paper and shoved it back in my pocket.

Jenny emerged from the cabin and stood at the top of the companionway wearing her lifejacket and holding mine out to me. "Right," I said, "seagoing rules, lifejackets on." She checked the dog's tether as I slipped quickly into my lifejacket. We passed down the eastern side of Portland Isle and cruised easily round the Bill, gaining nearly two knots of speed from the favourable tide as we passed the big red and white lighthouse. I picked up the binoculars and trained them on the National Coastwatch Lookout Station on the high ground up behind the lighthouse and was surprised to see someone peering back down at us through an enormous roof-mounted telescope. "Someone to watch over me," I thought, and whistled the tune of the old song.

As we settled onto a westerly heading with Portland growing smaller behind us, one little incident bothered me and disturbed my enjoyment of the cruise. An empty plastic tumbler fell from the binnacle onto the deck and as I bent to pick it up, my mobile phone fell from the top pocket of my shirt and skittered across the cockpit, making purposefully for the small open gap in the transom. I turned to pounce on it and for the first time noticed an increase in the wind strength. It had also moved around to almost due east and was blowing in over the port quarter. I glanced at the electronic wind indicator and was shocked to see that the wind speed was up to eighteen knots. That did not accord with what was written on the paper in my pocket so I puzzled over it for a while. Jenny mentioned that we had white horses astern of us and we chatted for a while about the forecast and the generally perceived incompetence of weather forecasters; but all the while my thoughts kept returning, unbidden, to that innocuous little remark at the end of the weather report.

Over the next hour the wind stayed steady from the same direction but the speed began to inch up a little, so that by the time I went below to log our position on the chart at twelve miles from Portland Bill, it was blowing at a steady twenty knots, gusting twenty-three. As I emerged back into the cockpit I noticed another change in the weather. Although it

17

was still warm and sunny, the humidity had begun to rise. Rising humidity and increasing wind from no obvious cause can be a sign of approaching thunderstorms; but I convinced myself that I was overreacting.

Ten minutes later Jenny nudged my arm and pointed over the front of the spray hood. "Look at that!" she said. I looked in the direction she was pointing. The horizon was slowly being obscured from the south by a line of low dark grey cumulus type clouds. I said nothing for a moment but as I watched the still forming cloud line ahead, I became acutely conscious of a further rise in humidity whenever I was out of the wind. I glanced down at the wind indicator which was now registering a persistent twenty-seven knots, and I realised that the movement of the boat was becoming uncomfortable with the rising sea beating on the transom. I decided to alter course to put the sea further round on the quarter and as I did so I realised that we needed to shorten sail. To take in a reef sensibly, I would need to turn the boat fully around into the wind; and when looking at the angry, short, steep-sided waves chasing us, I did not much fancy that manoeuvre. I turned once more so that the wind was almost right astern and, with much heaving and straining, began to roll in the big furling genoa until it was down to about a quarter. Jenny started the engine and silently handed me my oilskin jacket.

I turned twenty degrees to port which put the wind and sea on to a more comfortable bearing, on the port quarter. With the wind now over thirty knots, a full force seven, I decided to take out the autopilot and steer by hand. As I did so I glanced ahead and was shocked by what I saw. The bank of cloud had spread from horizon to horizon and had turned a dark, threatening purple.

"Look at that!" said Jenny, pointing towards the cloud. We both stared in silence as the purple band of cloud became thicker and more menacing. What she was actually pointing at was sudden bursts of illumination from within the cloud, signifying an electrical storm of some intensity. I could still see some blue sky above the bank of cloud but this was fast disappearing as the tops of the boiling thunderheads groped up into the troposphere. I tried to weigh up what we should do. The closest port of refuge was probably West Bay but to get there would put a nearly force eight wind right on the beam, and anyway the approach to West Bay was supposed to be difficult in a strong easterly.

The choice was to force on, risking a broach or worse, or to turn back, keeping a safer but slower course with the wind and waves on the nose. I briefly considered heaving-to although my competent but lightly-built Beneteau thirty-three footer had never liked that. The radio suddenly squawked a call from a lifeboat answering somebody's 'Mayday' call, I presumed from somewhere up ahead. That convinced me. We would turn.

We checked our lifejackets and our tethers securing us to the boat and I began the turn. I looked behind, trying to identify a reasonable patch between the waves, but they were short and steep and there wasn't much. Attempting to judge the point at which we would be beam on to the sea I started the turn to port, gently at first; then, as we began to roll heavily to starboard, I straightened the turn and opened the throttle. We charged at a forty-five degree angle into the next wave but the roll to starboard, which had passed seventy degrees, was beginning to ease. I saw the bow pitch high into the air but the turn was almost complete. Then the rain came and the daylight disappeared.

19

It was weird. Neither of us spoke and our faithful retriever sat immobile on the 'high side' cockpit seat. The daylight had gone completely; the rain was sheeting down and running in rivers from my oilskin jacket. Jenny was tucked up under the spray hood which protected her a little. Visibility seemed to vary between forty and a hundred yards. The sea was a confused maelstrom with wind and waves seemingly coming from every direction but never together. The wind in particular seemed to be constantly shifting and the noise blocked out everything else. *Iolanthe* was a sound boat but she was taking a pounding. I had dropped the mainsail as we completed the turn and this was now mostly within the sail pack cover with about the last six feet of sail stubbornly clinging to the mast and flapping to the wind. All around us we could see lightning and hear almost constant thunder. Sometimes the lightning actually hit the sea nearby, with an eye-searing flash and a noise like tearing silk. The boat was rearing and diving like a wild horse; and at the top of particularly steep waves, I could hear the propeller breaking surface and, as we surfed down the reverse side, I expected the boat to bury its nose deep into the oncoming wave. It never happened. Although the seawater climbed to be level with the deck, it was always stopped at that point.

We drove on with the storm screaming around us and the wind now up to sixty knots; but the boat was holding up well and I was able to maintain a course and even make some progress. I was wondering whether the storm would pass over us or just keep us locked in it for ever when there was an almighty bang. We had been hit by lightning. The only electronic item operating was the radio which gave out a blast of static and died. But when I looked down at the steering compass, I saw it was also wrecked. The card seemed to be spinning aimlessly and the instrument was useless. I said to myself, "I don't need this."

Jenny was peering anxiously towards me. She knew something was wrong but she didn't know what. She reached out a wet hand and I leaned over the wheel till our fingers touched. It gave me strength and I felt that if I could just keep heading the worst of the waves we would find our way out of this. My problem was that the waves were constantly changing direction and in the cocoon of ethereal darkness that now surrounded us I had nothing to refer to so I had no real idea of which way we should go. I was privately beginning to worry.

Then I saw the fin. I had to look hard, look away and back again before I believed what I was looking at. When I did look back there were two of them, almost side by side, swimming parallel with the boat about thirty feet away, with their bodies just below the surface. The fins were grey and the second one was curled over a little at the top. I turned back to the task of trying to steer the boat and then risked another glance to my left. There were now three fins, close together and all three much closer to the boat. I shouted into the gale towards Jenny and waved my arm to port. She followed my direction and I could see that she had seen them.

I looked back towards our new companions once more; and as I looked, I saw first one then a second head curve above a wave, each followed by a surprisingly big body; and I swear they were both looking directly at me. I felt the boat fall off a few degrees to starboard, corrected it and glanced back towards the dolphins. They had gone. Then I felt a distinct bump and – assuming it to be a wave – I corrected into it until my gaze was caught by Jenny excitedly pointing towards the bow. She stood and shouted to me, "They are pushing against the bow!" The third dolphin emerged high on a wave alongside the

21

cockpit and rolled to his right, nudging alongside the boat. I was amazed. Although the storm still raged around us I had all but forgotten it and my attention was riveted on what was happening in the sea alongside my boat. The three big animals were working assiduously to push the bows of the boat around to starboard. *Iolanthe* began to conform to the will of the dolphins; and when we appeared to have turned through about forty degrees to starboard, they seemed to be content and fell in alongside the port side of the bow, occasionally dropping back to the cockpit and sometimes giving the bow a nudge to starboard.

This extraordinary performance continued for the next three hours. The rain stopped but I didn't notice; and the thick grey cloud began to lift and thin. The dolphins stayed with us like faithful hunting dogs, sometimes on the starboard side but mostly curling through the waves close to port. But it began to dawn on me that they were much more than that. We were lost and at the mercy of the elements when they had come to our rescue and taken charge.

A brief ragged tear in the low cloud suddenly exposed the familiar shape of the Portland Bill lighthouse about two miles away on the port bow. I realised that two of our dolphin team were gently pushing the bow to starboard so I kept the wheel amidships and let them control our direction. Half an hour later the East Shambles Buoy lay close to port and the dolphin team had formed up, one on each side of the bows but keeping about a yard clear. The third animal, the smallest of the three, was out in front, like a pathfinder, marking the way.

The storm was at last beginning to abate and I realised that Jenny and I had both been mesmerised into silence. What we had seen and experienced was extraordinary. I recalled stories of dolphins helping shipwrecked mariners and I knew they were intelligent; but in this case they had quite literally turned up and saved us from the tempest.

We turned towards the familiar waters of Weymouth Bay and the dolphins, their work now done, began to cavort and leap alongside the boat. As we turned to the north, I ventured to hoist the mainsail so we turned once more into a now benign wind and I held the boat there while we hoisted the sail. I dropped the winch handle into its holder and turned to look over the port side. A huge grey dolphin was lying alongside the boat looking up at me with one big eye. Jenny appeared with the camera and I snapped off a picture. I am sure our aquatic saviour smiled.

We sailed slowly up towards Weymouth Harbour, having abandoned our voyage to Torquay, and the three dolphins accompanied us all the way. As we were slowly passing Portland Harbour breakwater they dropped away astern; and just when we thought we had seen the last of them, they came racing fast, one after the other, up the port side of the boat, each one in turn pulling up into a spectacular leap just a few feet away from the cockpit. Each leap was different and the last one was a one-and-a-half turn backward somersault, which we had only ever seen previously in an aquatic display.

Our three friends stayed with us to the harbour entrance before turning away to starboard, swimming in fast formation and leaping in perfect unison as they passed the cockpit. We wanted to wave. We never saw them again. But I have a photograph.

The Flight

She had been dozing. Drifting in and out of the shallow borders of sleep, lulled by the steady drone of the big Lycoming engine, as the small plane forged on through the warm tropical night air. But suddenly she was awake. Something had alerted her, something had changed; but as yet she did not know what it was.

She scanned the instruments. One or two of the small bulbs providing illumination to the panel had failed and so she used a torch, running it carefully over the flight instruments and then the engine temperatures and pressures. All seemed to be well so she slipped the torch back into the leg pocket of her flying suit and wriggled herself around against the seat straps to find a more comfortable position. She had been airborne now for over six hours and if her navigational calculations were accurate she should come within radio range of her mid-ocean destination within another two hours.

She reached down into the other leg pocket and pulled out the folded chart on which her departure point, track and destination were marked. It didn't offer her anything more than she already knew so she concentrated once more on carefully checking the flight instruments. The airspeed indicator showed one hundred and twenty knots and the altimeter, on a setting of 1013 millibars, declared that the aircraft had not deviated from the altitude of six thousand feet. The magnetic compass pointed steadily due east.

Content that all was well, she allowed herself to relax – but not too much. Then it happened. It must have been what had woken her a few minutes earlier. The engine missed a beat. It was not much, just a single hiccup coming from one of the thirty-two cylinders; nevertheless, she was concerned. It couldn't be icing because the outside air temperature gauge was showing sixty-eight degrees Fahrenheit. Maybe it was fuel – the mixture must be too weak, she thought; so she eased the fuel mixture lever forward a little. It would mean that fuel was being used at a faster rate but there was plenty in reserve; and the sacrifice of a little extra fuel was acceptable if it put her mind at rest on this, one of the longest legs on her attempt to fly around the world. The small aircraft flew on under a cloud haze which just failed to hide the shape of the three-quarter moon.

Despite her intention to the contrary, the droning engine, the long and tiring hours gone by and the warm cockpit once again began to ease her towards sleep. But the aircraft woke her up again. This time she jerked into sudden and alarmed wakefulness. The steady engine note had changed to an intermittent grumble, returning to a steady beat for perhaps a minute, then beginning the ragged rumble once more. She increased the mixture again but this only seemed to make the engine run even rougher. Fiddling with the mixture lever did seem to give some respite but there was now no doubt that the engine was running roughly most of the time, and it seemed to be losing power.

For the first time since she had started flying she experienced a frisson of fear. But she was determined. She had come so far on so many trips that she was not going to give in easily. She thrust the tendril of fear to the back of her mind and began to apply logic to her situation. It had to be a fuel problem, she thought, probably a blocked or blocking filter. But in these circumstances each filter had an emergency by-pass valve so that when the flow began to slow due to a

25

blockage the fuel would be re-routed. It couldn't be icing but it could be water in the fuel. She switched tanks and the problem seemed to ease. Then as she dared to relax, the grumbling discordant note started up again. This time the power loss was more pronounced and she realised that she would have to look for somewhere to set the aircraft down.

The plane was an amphibian, fitted with floats for water landing but with a wheel set in the centre of each float which could be lowered for a conventional grass or runway landing. The rough running had by now become really pronounced and the speed of the aircraft had dropped to little more than seventy knots. She had to keep the nose below the horizon even to maintain this speed; and consequently the altimeter now read three thousand feet with a steady rate of descent of three hundred feet per minute. At this rate she would land or crash within ten minutes.

The engine stopped, leaving the propeller windmilling in the slipstream. The speed dropped further. The rate of descent increased. She peered ahead through the windscreen which was now spotted with dark blobs of oil. Looking down behind the trailing edge of the wing, she tried to make out the wave pattern on the surface of the sea. She realised that she would have to attempt an open water landing and if the sea state was slight, if she could judge the height properly as she approached touchdown, and if she could land into the run of the sea, she might have a chance. But there were too many 'ifs'.

With a thousand feet to go – if the altimeter reading was correct – she twisted around in her seat to make sure the inflatable dinghy handle was within reach. Then she took the four flares and two smoke floats from the pocket in the door and stuffed them into the leg pockets of her flying suit. She tightened the seat harness as much as she could and peered ahead into the blackness. As she did so something caught her eye away to starboard. She looked away, fearing hallucination, and then deliberately looked back. There was a broken white line which seemed to be between her and what appeared to be the natural horizon. She eased the stick over to bring the now sluggish aircraft around in a gentle turn until the line of surf – it could be nothing else – stretched across from left to right in front of her.

Additionally she realised with rising hope that she could now discern a darkened land mass rising marginally above the horizon, outlined in the diffused moonlight. She mouthed an unfamiliar prayer. She was going to be all right. As she reached this conclusion, she realised that if she had been following the course she had set there could be no possibility of land in this part of the ocean. Her flight plan had been worked out carefully and independently checked; so either she was a long way off her predicted track or this was an uncharted island. The latter prospect seemed very unlikely indeed, which meant she was lost.

As the aircraft continued to descend towards the line of white surf her mind floated through the possibilities – a compass error, or possibly a radical wind change that had not been detected. With a shake of her head she dismissed such thoughts. The cause of her position error did not matter and did not affect the engine failure. That was a special problem all of its own. She needed to concentrate on landing the aircraft.

The surf line was now much closer and in the thin starlight she believed she could see placid water beyond the bright white line. But the aircraft's speed had dropped away and to avoid a stall she had to push the nose down a bit. The speed began to increase marginally, but so did the rate of descent. The little needle on the instrument was pointing stubbornly towards the cockpit floor. The altimeter indicated three hundred feet and the surf line was still ahead of the aircraft, moving – oh so slowly – towards her. She purposely ignored the altimeter indication, which was very likely wrong because the barometric pressure would have changed. Peering ahead through the windscreen and down through the right hand window, now with better night vision, she tried to assess the conundrum of height and distance. It was going to be tight, very tight. She eased the control column back a fraction, trying desperately to stretch the glide sufficiently to clear the surf which was now very close.

At last, by a miracle it seemed, the line of surf flashed past barely sixty feet below the aircraft. She allowed a long breath of relief to escape as she tightened the grip of her right hand on the control column, while her left hand, working by touch and long familiarity, darted around the cockpit, closing the throttle and mixture lever, switching off the battery master and magnetos, tightening straps and finally banging the door jettison lever.

Having cleared the reef, the water beyond seemed placid. The island, if that is what it was, was now strongly outlined as a break in the skyline; but she had no eyes for this. Her whole being was focussed on bringing down the aircraft as smoothly as possible. There seemed to be very little wind so there was no sideways drift but the landing would be fairly fast.

She consciously relaxed her tension, deliberately loosening the grip of her fingers on the control column as the aircraft eased down smoothly towards the surface of the water. She was braced and ready for the sudden deceleration as the water surface clutched at the floats, but the machine seemed to drift on and on, using the cushion of air beneath the wings to reduce the final descent.

At last the floats touched the surface simultaneously and she was thrown forward against the seat straps as the deceleration began. She breathed out and relaxed. As she did so the starboard float struck a small, conical rock, so small that it was only able to breach the surface during the trough of each tiny passing wave. But that was enough to make the rock into a killer. As the wooden float struck the rock head on at about forty knots, the lightweight structure of the float shattered. The aircraft was wrenched viciously around to the right. Before she could correct it, the port wing lifted into the air, tipping the whole aircraft to starboard, while it continued to spiral in the same direction. The starboard wing hit the surface and dug in, before snapping off halfway to the fuselage. The propeller, now windmilling without power, hit the water and shattered. With the remaining momentum the aircraft seemed to climb away from the water surface and then began to cartwheel towards the shore, snapping off bits of wing, tail and undercarriage as it did so. Despite the straps holding her in her seat, she was shaken around inside the cockpit until consciousness vanished and she knew no more.

****

The sun was hot. She opened one eye and then shut it again. She could feel her face burning as well as unidentifiable pain from her lower legs. She sensed that she was wet and half of her body seemed cool. Carefully and methodically she started to move, first her fingers, then her hands, then each arm. There were pains everywhere but mostly from her lower legs. After perhaps ten or fifteen minutes she opened both eyes and realised she was lying on her back in water. Her arm movements were restricted by the inflated lifejacket and she was lying on alternately warm and cool sand, half in and half out of the water. She attempted to use her elbows to drag her body further out from the waterline. The pain came again, much stronger this time, and she passed out. Presently she woke again. Slowly, ever so slowly she tried to repeat the manoeuvre and this time, although the pain came once more, it seemed less intense.

When she was clear of the water she ventured to prop herself up on her elbows so she could see what surrounded her. There was nothing except calm blue-green water, a white streak marking the position of the reef in the distance and a few bits and pieces of wood, canvas and other flotsam. Realising that this was all that was left of her beloved aeroplane that had carried her so far and had been her home, she began silently to weep. A beach of fine white sand stretched away to the left and right and a gentle noise behind her suggested a light breeze mingling with some sort of vegetation.

She lay back with hands over her face for a few minutes, hoping to gather strength so she could try to move further up the beach and maybe gain some shelter. She did not bother to cry out because, without any tangible evidence to the contrary, she was certain that she was alone on the beach and on the island.

It took an hour and a half to cover the eight yards from the waterline to the first vegetation. This proved to be tussocks of coarse grass, in several cases raised a foot above the sand. More struggling produced a place where she could sit, but this seemed to increase the pain in her lower left leg. She looked briefly at the track she had made from the water's edge and was horrified to see that the second half of the indented track

30

was decorated with a trail of blood – her blood. The pain in her leg had by now become dulled and was competing with the burning skin of her face. She still wore her inflated lifejacket, for the simple reason that she could not move sufficiently to take it off.

Dragging the rest of her body up onto the grass she lay back, cushioning her head on the inflated rubber, and slept. The tropical twilight was very short and the darkness of the night was complete within ten minutes of the sun dropping below the horizon. Half an hour after the darkness, the land crabs came. They came in ones and twos at first and scuttled nervously around the strange body stretched on the grass. The first forays of the smaller crabs were to parts of the body clothed in jacket and flying overalls. As they touched the fabric, each one recoiled, driven away by the alien scent of oil, rubber and heavy cotton.

Later, bigger crabs arrived. And these were bolder. One after another they advanced, principal claw extended, pincers snapping expectantly. Still, the body lay unmoving and the number, size and variety of crabs increased.

She was dreaming, or so she thought. But then, with a scream, she realised that this was no dream. Despite the pain she jerked upright, scattering the smaller crabs that had been climbing over her recumbent form. There was pain from her other leg which she realised with horror was caused by the pincers twisting into her flesh. She flailed about her in the darkness, smashing her hands down on the shells, hurling fistfuls of sand and flinging crabs away from her. They seemed excited by the battle and came back to her with renewed vigour.

As she scrabbled more and more desperately in the sand, she felt something more solid under the fingers of her left hand. She jerked at it. It moved. She pulled again and in a small shower of white sand it came free. It was a length of stick about two inches across and thirty inches long. She had a weapon. Desperately she started to hammer down at where she thought the crabs were and despite not being able to see them easily she realised that she was hitting her targets. She developed a technique of grabbing crabs which had reached her body, flinging them down beside her and smashing the place with her makeshift club.

Her watch had gone so she had no idea of the time; but it must have been over an hour before her enemy withdrew.

During the day she moved further under the shade of the bushes and slept. As the sun dropped towards the horizon she moved herself to try to establish a more defensive position. Nevertheless the crabs came in numbers, just as they had on the first night. The same thing happened on the third and fourth nights, by which time she was becoming very weak from lack of food, from her injuries and from loss of blood.

On the fifth morning, when she had painfully and slowly manoeuvred herself into a semi-seated position, propped against the grass bank at the edge of the beach, she was peering across the lagoon through slitted eyes when she thought she detected a movement. She looked again, turned away, then peered once more; and the movement was still there.

While she nurtured her conviction that she was hallucinating, the distant blobs turned themselves into three outrigger canoes. She stared peacefully and unbelievingly towards them as they came, in line abreast, towards the beach. The canoes grounded on the sand and the occupants jumped out into the shallow water, gathering round and dragging each outrigger further onto the sand. Although she had not moved, shouted or signalled, they knew she was there. They walked purposefully towards her and stood in a half circle facing her. There were five men and

32

two women. The men were dressed only in ragged shorts or short skirt-like garments and the women were enshrouded in all-enveloping robes. One man, older and shorter than the others, seemed to be the leader. He leaned on a wooden staff and peered at her, staring through brown, leathery wrinkled skin. She sat, silent, looking back at him impassively, acutely aware of her vulnerability and the smell of her sweat and her injuries. She believed they would kill her and she was resigned to this.

To her surprise, the small man started to speak, gesticulating with his staff towards where she lay. She could not understand him but realised clearly that he was giving orders. Two men stepped towards her and, with no effort, one of them picked her up in his arms while the other one gathered up her stick, a flying glove and a boot. She was carried down towards the boats and laid gently in the shade cast by the centre one. She squinted up as another pair of brown hands appeared, this time clutching a long fat green frond which appeared to have been cut from a cactus plant – but without the usual spines.

The hands produced a knife. Here it comes, she thought; but instead of advancing on her, the knife was being used to cut slices across the long leaf. Each slice was then opened, exposing a milk-white fluid. The opened sections were then applied to her face, smearing the jelly-like fluid across her raw and blistered skin. The effect was remarkable. Almost immediately, the burning sensation disappeared and was replaced by a cool balmy feeling. She imagined her parched skin drinking in the fluid to repair the ravages of the sun. Other hands were now working on the burns on the exposed skin of her arms and legs. Then her attention was suddenly wrenched away as someone was attempting to move her injured leg. She screamed. They were trying to set her broken bone, working it and aligning it to the other leg before tying the two limbs tightly together against a padding of mud, grass and leaves placed between them. The pain came in waves greater than before and she fainted.

When she woke again her first sensation was one of movement. She was being gently rocked and the pain had receded. She was in a boat – one of the canoes, she realised. The boat was rocking gently as it skimmed through the water. In front of her was a brown back and, looking up, she could see a brown sail which was heavily patched and looked as though it was made of canvas or cotton. She realised that she was lying in a bed formed of fresh fish, some of which were still alive. The smell of fish was strong but for the first time since her engine had stopped, she felt content. All through the process of rescue, as she now thought of her experiences at the hands of these strange people, none of them had attempted to communicate with her.

It took three days for the three canoes to reach their home island and when they ground up onto the beach, one after another, the whole village turned out to meet them. Children clustered around as they lifted the injured woman gently from among the fish and carried her up the beach into the shade and coolness of a long palm-leaf roofed hut. Still no one had spoken.

****

She lived with the fishing people for nearly thirty years. During all that time only the women of the tribe spoke to her; so when she learned their language, it was the language of the women, a working, cleaning, cooking language; but she was happy. When she died the whole tribe turned out and reverently carried her body into the interior to be placed on a platform raised six feet above the grass and wild flowers, as was their custom.

The clear water rippled in the reflection along the side of the big white-hulled yacht. Harry sat in the cockpit, puzzling over charts and the screens of two small black boxes. One of these was giving the yacht's position from the Global Positioning System satellites circling high above the earth. The other screen was a Chart Plotter, also based on information from the GPS system. Harry was puzzled. "Honey, according to everything I know it shouldn't be here," he called down to the saloon.

"What shouldn't be here?" A woman's voice floated out from the companionway.

"It – the whole thing. The whole island," replied Harry.

A tall brown-skinned woman emerged languorously from the hatchway. "Well, somebody knows the island should be here," she said. "Look at all the junk we found." She poked a set of red painted toenails towards the pile of barnacle and coral-encrusted pieces of metal that littered the cockpit and the side deck.

Harry swept the Admiralty chart to one side, moved towards his wife and, rummaging among the bits and pieces in front of her, he picked up a roughly circular lump. "That is the hub of a wheel," he said. He moved his hands among the other pieces of encrusted metal and wood. Picking up and moving several items, he pointed to them, "Spark plugs, a piece of propeller boss, wiring, glass-surfaced instruments," he said. "I tell you, an aircraft must have crashed here."

"Yes, dear," said his wife, "but I expect it was a long time ago. Shall we swim again, or do you want to eat?"

The Voyage – a Space Odyssey

The launch had been routine. A veteran of more than twenty Super-Shuttle launches and with almost six months of time in space, or as the geeks at the new mission control centre in the Nevada Desert would have it, "time in near earth orbit", Carl considered himself not only a space veteran but also a master of his trade.

Carl hovered in near zero gravity in front of the communications screen, which was now filled with an urgent signal from the Super-Shuttle launch centre in Florida. Flashing orange lights at the four corners of the screen indicated that the signal was sufficiently urgent to merit an "Immediate" precedence as well as a "Secret" security classification. The signal said, in unexplained stark terms that the launch of the Super-Shuttle *Orbiter Nine* would be delayed by five days. Carl sighed to himself. Added to the existing gap between launches this would mean that he and the first half of the Project Mars crew would be waiting with increasing boredom for nearly two weeks before they could finally assemble the interstellar vehicle and begin the great journey out into the near solar system. Carl propelled himself through the empty crew capsule into the control room where the other two men and one woman in his half of the crew waited.

In fact only Yuri was awake. The other two hung inverted from the sleep brackets. Carl showed the flimsy print-out to Yuri, his second-in-command. "Shit," said Yuri, displaying his expanding command of colloquial English. "Couldn't organise a vucking piss-up in a vucking vodka vactory."

"Want a game of 'Mind'?" Carl thought there was no point in dwelling on other men's failings. It was bad for morale. Yuri wasn't interested in playing 'Mind' so Carl pressed the red game switch on his remote compufone and waited while a virtual screen drifted into his cone of vision. Carl played through the varying degrees of difficulty until sleep overcame him and he floated away into a corner by the second observation hatch. The crew stayed in near suspended animation until the auto-sleep guidance system cut in and lowered the oxygen content of the space station's life capsule, easing the four astronauts into minimum activity mode. They slept for the next four days.

The automatic systems of the second international space station gradually shut down all non-essential facilities to minimum life support level while the ungainly space station moved into medium level earth orbit and greedily sucked in energy every time it passed through solar illumination.

Two hundred miles below, the huge steel and Carbomin plates covering the rocket launch silos had begun to slide to one side, exposing the nose cones of the two rockets and their associated booster motors. As the desert sun began to reflect from the metal and the polished Carbomin surfaces, the four man crew of the primary vehicle completed their final preparations, picked up their life support modules and moved slowly, in single file, across the metal bridge and in through the hatch set in the side of the launch vehicle. The reserve crew had also been kitted up and were now waiting in the underground ready room, mildly hoping that *Orbiter Nine* would fail to launch, thus giving them the opportunity to enter the lists of Space Heroes. They were to be disappointed.

The final count proceeded steadily and without hitch; and after three hours, steam began to emerge from the silo, signifying the final stage of the launch procedure.   As the steam cleared, the familiar muffled roar of the igniting rockets blanked out all other sound.   The main nose cone, then the smaller nose cones of the four boosters, emerged from the open silo, peeping briefly into the harsh sunlight before accelerating, first to clear the silo entrance and then, with the main motor adding thrust, the whole six-storey high rocket system soared away into the pale sky.   Within seconds it was just a pinpoint on the end of a twisting column of smoke.

As *Orbiter Nine* began to shake off earth's gravity, the space station computers, detecting the successful launch from earth, began to bring their systems back to fully operational mode and the crew started to wake, refreshed, re-energised and hungry.   Wake-meals were quickly sucked from the small capsules attached to each support belt and, without preamble, they started work.

The routine preparations for interplanetary travel had been practised so often that they were fixed within the frontal lobes of the crew members.   Nevertheless they followed the required procedures, working in two-person teams and checking everything against the cards, calling actions as they were completed so that the preparation process was automatically picked up by the monitors and displayed on the bridge screens. Any missed operation or even an operation out of sequence would cause an alarm buzzer to sound throughout the space station and within each suit.   No alarms were heard.

Carl floated across to the Comcen and spoke towards the screen.   *"Orbiter Nine,* this is *Orbiter Five,* station docked.   I see your launch; confirm Ops Normal."

"Ops Normal."   Instantly the screen spoke back to him. Despite all his training to avoid and control emotion, Carl could not resist a thrill of anticipation tingling through his body.　The remaining crew were on their way.　The great adventure was about to begin.　Man was setting out to travel to another planet and land there for the first time.

It took only thirty hours for *Orbiter Nine* to reach medium earth orbit and align with *Orbiter Five*.　Forty-five earth minutes later, the two giant rockets were docked side by side on the space station, the two men and two women of the arriving crew section had transferred to the Control Centre, and work had begun to dismantle the sections of the rockets required to complete the construction of the inter-planetary spaceship.

From now on the crew worked like the automatons they had been trained to be.　Although between them they represented four nationalities and three races, they worked and communicated as one.　Forty-eight earth hours after the arrival of *Orbiter Nine*, the spaceship was finally assembled and ready to leave for the planet Mars.　At this point the crew of the spaceship were able to rest while banks of computers on earth checked everything they had done and other computers checked the checkers.　Nothing was to be left to chance.

"Ground Control, we are ready for launch."　There was a delay of two minutes before the words emerged from the speakers in the control room deep below the desert.

"Ground Control will now assume call sign Earth Control."　The words tumbled from the wall speakers and simultaneously from the integral headset speakers.

"Roger that," responded Carl, automatically.

"Standby to launch from orbit.　Ignition will be initiated from Earth Control. Acknowledge. Over."

"Roger," said Carl, looking around to see that his crew were all in their assigned seats.　There was no need to strap in because the initial thrust forces should be light.

"Standby! Ten, nine, eight, seven, six ..." The spaceship, for that is what it had become, juddered as the securing clamps released their hold and the ship rested free but unmoving alongside the Space Station.

The countdown continued: "five, four, three ..." A single motor fired and the spaceship began to glide away from the International Space Station, rather like an electric train starting to move. At "two" and "zero" the next two motors fired. All three would burn for only twelve minutes, boosting the spaceship to escape velocity so that it could break away entirely from Earth's gravity.

The speakers started again: "God bless you, and grant you a safe journey, *Endurance*." Nobody replied because they were all concentrating on the screens before them.

A few minutes later Carl spoke. "We have breakout velocity, Earth. We are on our way."

"Go to Mars and good luck," came the answer. The ship began to angle away from Earth and as it did so the auto-environment began to change the lighting, oxygen supply and temperature in the craft, gradually sending the entire crew into a deep sleep which would last for thirty days while units within their suits would feed them intravenously.

The planet Mars follows an elliptical orbit which allows the distance from earth to vary between two hundred and fifty million miles and just thirty-six million miles at the closest point. The optimum launch date had occurred when the red planet was actually forty-five million miles from the earth, with the gap progressively increasing. The newly named spacecraft *Endurance* would be able to increase its speed by measured bursts from its booster motors, aiming first towards the moon, before passing close around the outer side of the moon. This manoeuvre would enable the spaceship to further increase its velocity to the equivalent of almost fifty thousand earth miles per hour. It had been predicted that this would enable the ship to enter orbit around Mars in about one hundred and twenty-eight days.

In order to preserve fuel, oxygen and water, a plan had been developed whereby the crew would be mildly sedated, sufficiently to enable them to remain in a prolonged state of sleep. As the ship accelerated towards Earth's moon, the eight men and women had already entered the first somnolent period of ten days.

By the time the astronauts began to emerge from their prolonged rest period the ship had been guided, by its automatic systems, past and around the moon, accelerating close to its cruising speed. The next three days were to be spent in a gentle process of system checks, communicating with Earth Control, feeding and following an exercise regime. By the time they were settling into the second sleep period they had completed a third of their voyage. Everything checked out and everything was going well.

It was day seventy-two when the first problem occurred. The astronauts were all asleep, tethered in or above their assigned sleeping spaces, when the ship began to shake, accompanied by a rattling noise reminiscent of being sprayed with gravel. The unusual motion and noise triggered the shutdown of the sleep system. Carl was the first to wake, followed by computer engineer Sally Streamer. No words passed between them as Carl tried to settle the uncontrolled movement and Sally checked rapidly through the various computer systems. The noise eased and then died away completely. The movement of the craft was progressively reduced until it was no more than a gentle weave on either side of the set course. The two astronauts visibly relaxed as they

41

began to be joined by their colleagues, each of whom set about attending to their particular duties, once again with very little dialogue between them.

Carl composed a carefully recorded signal to Earth Control, reporting what had happened and giving a concise but detailed statement of their present situation. It took nearly forty minutes before the burst transmission completed its journey through empty space and into the atmosphere of Earth. An acknowledgement was sent which arrived back at the spacecraft after a further fifty minutes. As the green light of the signalled reply was tracking across the communications screen, the spaceship began to roll slowly onto its starboard side, turning forty degrees away from the set course at the same time. The occupants didn't feel the movement but they were alerted by the movement of the stars seen through the observation ports.

Carl decided to defer the second rest period while he and his crew worked to correct the attitude and course of the ship. By the time they had completed their various tasks and settled to relax and consume a space meal, their destination was hugely evident through two of the starboard-side observation ports. Carl was worried about the unexplained random movements of the spacecraft and he decided it was time to discuss the problem and their response with his crew.

"Can anybody offer any reason at all for the malfunctions?" Carl gazed at the men and women grouped in the air and on the deck in front of him.

"Maybe it was not a malfunction." Psychiatrist Raymond Liu spoke slowly, enunciating each word carefully.

"What do you mean?" Emerald Yeboah looked frightened. She stared hard at Raymond.

Yuri broke the silence that followed. "We didn't do it; Earth couldn't do it; there is no record of malfunction in the ship; so something else caused it."

Carl decided to interrupt the course the conversation was taking. "I think we should remain at cruising watch stations for at least the next forty-eight hours and if everything remains normal, then go into the final extended rest period." He spoke briskly and started to rise from his perch near the floor when he was interrupted by Raymond Liu.

"First," said Raymond, "everything is not normal. Second, we don't know why. Perhaps we should be thinking of aborting the mission."

Several voices chimed in at once. Carl turned towards the anxious faces. "One at a time!" he said.

Yuri was the first to speak. "There could be a simple explanation. To turn back would be a betrayal of everything we have prepared for."

Jean Lemaire, who had not spoken yet, raised his hand. "If we go on and do not survive, for whatever reason, we will achieve nothing," he said. "If we return we should be able to re-dock and preserve our experience and the ship." His deep voice with its mildly Gallic accent was bound to carry weight with his colleagues.

Caitlin started to speak. As she spoke, she ticked off her points on her fingers. "First," she said, "if we do cruise watches for another two Earth days, and then a full sleep pattern, we will be nearly at day ninety-six. At that point," she ticked off the second finger, "we will be approaching Mars orbit." She grasped her third finger. "Preparations for Mars orbit and let-down prior to launching the probe will take three days. It is too tight." She tilted her head back, challenging them to disagree.

43

Emerald, floating close to Caitlin, entered the conversation. "What do we think caused the initial noise?" she asked.

Carl thought for a moment. "Space dust?"

"Meteorites?" This came from Yuri. He answered his own question. "I do not think so," he mumbled ponderously.

"There is absolutely no record within the ship of striking any form of space debris, and if we had been struck, no matter how slightly, there would be a record." Jean Lemaire spoke again.

"Okay. We are discussing something that cannot happen yet, so I think there is little point," said Carl. Several heads nodded in agreement. He continued, "The only practical way of turning around this mission and returning to Earth is by going around Mars and working the same sling-shot manoeuvre as we did around the moon, so our only choice for the next twenty-four hours is to settle down to cruising watches and make our next decision in two days. Anybody disagree?" Several faces looked worried but nobody disagreed. They pulled themselves through the control room to their assigned places and began once more to go over and over their routine checks.

Nothing happened to disturb their routine during the cruising watch period. Mars grew progressively bigger and photographs, radiation and light readings were taken. After twenty-four hours a signal was sent back to Earth, which would now take much longer to arrive; and it was therefore likely that by the time any reply could be sent from earth the spaceship would already be entering Mars orbit.

With all systems responding normally, the crew entered rest mode for the last time before their final approach to Mars. But only eight days into the sleep period they were once again rudely awakened by a rattling noise on the hull, this time much

44

louder than before. One by one the crew awoke and moved towards their action stations. The noise grew louder. Then suddenly it stopped while the craft began to oscillate as it had previously. But this time, the oscillation was accompanied by sudden blinding lights from somewhere outside.

"What is it?" asked Sally.

"Something is trying to communicate with us." Carl was struggling to come to terms with what was taking place around his tiny but previously highly ordered world.

"Switch out the internal lights!" called Yuri as the rumble began again, though more subdued. "Answer their signal!" Carl, at the Master Station, obeyed, counted to five and then switched the internal lights on again.

At once a battery of light appeared to explode all around the now tumbling spacecraft. "Oh God!" The scream came from Emerald, floating near the after observation hatch. Jean Lemaire and Raymond Liu propelled themselves across the control room, peering out to where she was pointing.

A huge glowing spacecraft was paralleling their course not five hundred metres away. The size dwarfed the *Endurance* and a brilliant display of coloured lights was apparently emerging from somewhere on the surface of the craft. As they watched, they heard Yuri from the other side of the cabin yell, "Look at the size of that!"

What they did not see was what was behind them. As the Red Planet loomed massively beyond the forward hatch, darkness progressively overwhelmed them when the largest of the three alien spacecraft moved slowly forward and swallowed the *Endurance* through a great black opening where its nose cone should have been.

At Earth Control, they tried for over three months to re-establish communication with the *Endurance,* to no avail. All

45

that the operators received were occasional powerful bursts of plasma energy. Because they could not understand what they were or where they came from, they dismissed them.

If they had known the language and had been able to decipher the signals, they would have received the message: "They are safe."

A Walk in the Desert

Jack was frustrated and furious. He was mostly furious with himself. "How could anybody be so bloody stupid" He roared. He was standing by the side of the desert road and there was absolutely no-one to hear him so the only value in shouting was as a safety valve for his deep frustration. The desert stretched away on either side, bisected by the empty road gradually disappearing in a series of bizarre waving images to the eastern horizon.. There was no one to hear him. He kicked at the unresponsive German army motorcycle again.

It had seemed a good idea at six o'clock that morning to take the motorbike and set off along the main road to identify broken-down vehicles, note their positions and then be back at the main camp in Sidi Barani for a leisurely breakfast. If the lull in the fighting continued he could then send out the REME repair and recovery teams and maybe get the unit back to full vehicle establishment once more. Unfortunately this would probably mean having to return the huge rugged 'go anywhere' trucks he had borrowed from the American First Army.

He sat in the sand beside the road and waited. He felt stupid as thoughts crowded in to produce a long list of 'what-ifs' or might-have-beens'. After the unopposed landing in Algeria it had been a relatively straightforward run across North Africa in support of the rapidly moving front line. Sitting at the edge of the empty desert road, Jack reflected that it had also been a long time since he had last faced the enemy, on the approach to Dunkirk and he realized that despite continuous training he had forgotten some of the requirements of self-preservation in war.

The company had landed at Oran as one of a few British units attached to the United States 1st Infantry Division and the British Royal Army Service Corps trucks had rolled ashore some hours after the initial landing. Despite the setback when General George Patton's troops had run into one of Rommel's last hammer blows at Kasserine Pass, progress along the coastal strip of North Africa had been rapid – some would say, almost spectacular. Thousands of German and some Italian prisoners had been taken and Axis resistance was almost non-existent. The British 'wagoners' had been hard pressed to keep up with the rapidly moving front line units, bringing supplies forward and transporting prisoners to the rear. Now, only five months after the landings the Afrika Korps was squeezed between Montgomery's Eighth Army pressing forward from Egypt and The American First Army moving in rapidly from the west.

As Jack waited, the sun climbed higher, and he sweated. More than once he cursed his own stupidity for sauntering off on a recently captured motorbike and not even remembering to take his side-arm with him. What a laugh that would be when his men realised what their Company Sergeant Major had done – and he was the man who was always going on at them about being prepared for anything when facing the enemy, even if the enemy was nowhere to be seen.

He stared at the offending motorbike, now lying uselessly on its side and his thoughts returned to the moment it had come into his possession. It was only one week ago. It seemed more, but that was because time seemed to have stretched since they had rolled unopposed down the ramps of the landing craft into the shallow water of Oran.

The bike had belonged to a Wermacht Dispatch Rider only one week previously. He had been surprised by running into a six vehicle convoy, carrying food from Sidi Barani to the front line, which had been overtaken by one of the frequent and dense sandstorms that routinely hindered progress. The men were still huddled inside the cabs of their trucks but Jack had seen that the storm was easing and visibility was improving. He had just climbed stiffly down from the cab of the huge American truck and was standing on the new carpet of red sand covering the road when out of the gloom came the motorbike. The rider had been attempting to negotiate the thicker part of the storm and he was travelling at barely more than walking pace.

Jack hauled his Webley revolver out of its holster and loosed off a shot. The effect of this was to cause the motorbike rider to open the throttle wide, causing the back wheel of the machine to spin. He failed to correct the slide so bike and rider careered across the road into a small newly formed dune at the edge of the tarmac. The machine fell sideways and the rider was pitched into the sand. He scrabbled for the Luger strapped to his waist but gave up when he saw the barrel of the Webley pointed unwaveringly, only ten inches from his face.

"Hands Hocht!" yelled Jack in a mangle of languages.

The German looked crestfallen. He sat by his bike and slowly raised both hands. "Kamerad" he ventured tentatively.

"Kamerad, my arse!" Jack held the revolver pointed steadily at his prisoner. Then, without taking his eyes off the German, now in a crouched position beside his bike, Jack shouted to his men, who were just emerging from the sand-covered vehicles behind him "Get over here and secure Fritz – and get his bike loaded in the back of my truck."

More guns were pointed at the unfortunate German soldier, who dropped his own weapon on the sand. Jack kicked it a yard or so away. Corporal 'Taff' Thomas arrived with another man and a length of rope. The German was hauled to his feet and turned around so that his hands could be tied behind him. A rope was then used to hobble his ankles and led upward to be attached to the bound hands. It was going to be very difficult for the man to move.

As the corporal, now with two men, led the prisoner shuffling towards the back of the smaller one-ton truck, another couple of men pulled the motorbike upright and started pushing it towards the lead vehicle.

"Where you takin' my bike?" The German prisoner spoke in halting English as he turned to stare after the motorbike.

"Not your bike anymore," said Jack. "My bike now!"

"But I ride it all zhe way from Berlin" said the anguished prisoner in his longest burst of English yet.

Jack grinned as he placed the Webley carefully back in its holster, "well, Fritz," he said, "I am going to bloody well ride it all the way back again. Now shut up and forget it."

* * * * * * * * * *

The sun was becoming really hot now and there was very little wind. Jack examined his water canteen – silently thanking providence that at least he had remembered to bring that with him. He shook it, estimating that it was probably still half full and he took a small amount of water into his mouth, allowing it to swirl around his tongue and teeth before swallowing it. He pulled the scarf from around his neck, which he had worn as protection from the flying sand, and arranged it on top of his head, keeping his beret in place under it. Then he dragged himself up from the sand and levered the bike into an upright position. He contemplated having another try at getting the damn thing started but he had already tried everything. Instead he positioned the machine on its stand so that it stood

50

between him and the sun, now fairly high in the sky. The machine provided a small area of shadow and Jack pressed himself as closely into this as he could. He settled down to wait once more.

Three hours had now passed without a single vehicle appearing on the road from either direction. Jack was becoming seriously worried. A few days ago, this road had been busy with a steady flow of American and British Army traffic rumbling along in each direction. Jack drank the last few tepid drops of water from his canteen and wondered how long it would be before someone would venture out from the camp at Sidi Barani to look for him. He had been out of touch now for nearly five hours so he assumed someone must appear soon.

Someone did appear. But they were coming from the wrong direction, heading towards the camp rather than away from it. Nevertheless Jack felt relieved that at last he would be able to hitch a lift back to the camp. The German motorbike, he thought, could stay there and damn-well rot!

It was just a cloud of dust that emerged in the far distance on the arrow-straight road. Eventually, a shapeless blob could be discerned at the base of the dust cloud. Both blob and cloud were difficult to see because the images were so distorted by the waves of heat rising from the desert.

The blob formed itself into a vehicle. Then a few minutes later it became a car – a big car. Jack stood in the middle of the road where he could be seen plainly by the oncoming driver.

The vehicle began to slow down as it approached. Jack stood his ground and held up his right arm in the best "Military Police" style . Then, as the car cruised to a stop in front of him, Jack realised with shock that the vehicle was German. It was a big convertible Mercedes of the type favoured by senior

German officers. Although it was caked in the fine ochre-coloured desert sand, as it pulled to a halt in front of Jack's still upheld arm, he could clearly see the swastika symbols on the doors, as well as a small flag-shaped metal badge fixed to the front bumper, identifying the car as belonging to the Desert Air Force of the Luftwaffe.

Predominant among the thoughts now racing around in Jack's head was one that suggested he had just reached the end of his own personal line. There was nowhere to run to and he was already braced for the impact of the bullet that he was sure would be fired from the car.

No bullet came. Instead, a handsome, tanned and smiling face appeared from the front window. "Good day," said the German officer in almost faultless English. "We are looking for a British prisoner of war camp, where we can surrender. I wonder if you could tell us where we might find one?"

Another set of emotions flooded through Jack's head, but he was recovering his composure and was thinking quickly. "I can do better than that," he said. "I can show you if you like."

The smiling face turned in to the interior of the car and a short conversation took place in German. Jack thought, this is it. The bullet is coming anyway and it will be one more for the Fatherland. As he stood watching he became worryingly aware that each of the officers wore a polished leather belt with a very large holster attached. 'Lugers' he thought inconsequentially, and I've got bugger all!'

The conversation between the officers in the car ended abruptly and the smiling face was once more turned towards him.

"Yes" said the smiler. I have asked the Oberst and we think it is good that we take you with us and then you can show us the British camp. Not the American, of course." He paused, then continued with a knowing look in place of the smile, "And I think you would rather ride than walk, no?" At this there was a ripple of coarse laughter around the car. Jack suppressed a shiver and smiled weakly.

The wide door of the car was opened and the two men in the backseat began to shuffle round, creating a small space between them. Jack climbed into the car and squeezed himself into the space between the two officers. As he settled back, a hand was thrust towards him and the man on his right said "Leutnant Schmidt, Hans, yah?" Automatically Jack took the proffered hand and then turned to repeat the small formality with the man on his left.

The car began to move slowly ahead, leaving behind the dirty yellow dust cloud which had overtaken them. Jack's new companions smiled indulgently towards him, as he sat stiffly upright, wondering at the likelihood that he would not survive his present predicament.

The officer on his left broke the silence. "Zigarette?" he said, proffering a silver cigarette case almost full with American 'Lucky Strike' cigarettes.

At the same time, the man on his right spoke. "For us ze var iss over, jah?" Everyone laughed uproariously. Jack managed a rueful smile.

The car gathered speed quickly and Jack began to worry about the shell holes and breeches in the road that he had so carefully negotiated on the ill-fated motor-bike only a few hours ago. The Major driving the car seemed to be somewhat of a fatalist, swerving around some of the worst of the damaged road but crashing through other parts with audible protests from the suspension and bodywork of the big Mercedes. They continued like this for just over half an hour, their progress being marked by the shapes of smashed vehicles and burnt out tanks scattered into the far distance, shimmering and waving in the heat haze. Most of these seemed to lie to the south of the road, on the left hand of the speeding car. On the road there was no sign of any other moving vehicles. The two men in the front seats began to talk in German and then the Colonel, 'Herr Oberst', leaned over the back of his seat and addressed Jack.

"We stop for some lunch," he said. "Then we go to prison!" Everyone laughed as though the Oberst had cracked a hugely funny joke. Jack didn't laugh. He believed that as soon as the car pulled off the road he would be killed. 'It'll be one more for the Fatherland.' The thought returned to him unbidden and stuck in his mind. He thought of making a run for it as soon as he got out of the car, but there was nowhere to run to, just flat, featureless desert in every direction. The only break in the horizon surrounding the speeding vehicle was the huge yellow dust cloud, doggedly pursuing them and obscuring the road behind. Jack made up his mind to bolt in that direction.

At last the car began to slow down. Jack tensed for his escape attempt, but the driver pulled the car to the right and they swept off the road, crunching through a flattish area of gravel and small flat rocks. The dust cloud swept past them along the road before beginning to dissipate. Jack became resigned to his inevitable fate.

The car squeaked and wheezed to a stop on a patch of fine flat gravel and the German occupants hopped out immediately. Jack took his time. By the time he did get out of the car the boot lid was already open and the two 'leutnants' were unfolding a big canvas sheet. They hooked two corners of the sheet onto the side of the car and fixed the other two corners onto folding tripod posts, forming a small but effective shelter. Despite his intention to run, Jack just stood and watched. He was nudged as the major struggled past carrying a very big wicker hamper, followed by 'Herr Oberst', humming "Lilley Marlene" and carrying another folded canvas sheet together with a folding wooden camp stool.

Jack watched, mesmerised, as the Colonel-Oberst, still happily humming "Lilley Marlene", spread the canvas sheet on the gravel under the improvised shelter. He unfolded the small camp stool and perched himself on it, watching as the rest of his team completed their assigned tasks.

Within perhaps four minutes altogether, a picnic area had been set up beside the car and the contents of the hamper spread out on the canvas sheet. While the Colonel supervised proceedings from his small seat, the other three officers produced steel plates and cups as well as bottles of champagne, beer and water. Sliced ham, small pies, sausages, pickles, apples and a couple of long thin crusty loaves were also excavated from the hamper, followed finally by two small bottles of schnapps.

The colonel stood up and, smiling benignly, waved everyone into a seating position with one hand while the other clutched a steel cup. The others eased themselves down to kneel and sit on the fine gravel. One of the Germans perched himself on the running board of the car. Jack squatted beside the car as a steel cup was placed in his hand.

The colonel stood and waved his cup in the air. "A toast" he shouted, then "No, sit, sit, sit" as the men around him began to rise. They all resumed their positions. Mutely, Jack started to sit on the sand until the 'leutnant' on the running board indicated the space beside him on the rest of the car's running board. Jack sat there.

"To the end of ze var!" bawled the Colonel.

"To the end of the war," echoed the other three in rather better English.

"End of the war," echoed Jack, less stridently. He tipped the cup to his mouth and gasped as the fiery schnapps hit his throat.

"To the victorious British Army!" The Colonel was on his feet again. They all followed suit again , then following with toasts to the American Army, to the British Army, Montgomery, Rommel, the Luftwaffe, the Afrika Korps and individually to themselves.

"To our friend, the Oberfeldwebel Jaque!" Shouted the Major to the desert air.

"To the over-fed rebel" muttered Jack, trying vainly and hazily to reply and repeat the German words.

They made their toasting way through both bottles of schnapps, at least three bottles of champagne and some beer. Nearly two hours later, with the sun low in the south-western sky they all piled into the car once more, re-joined the road and set off, weaving erratically along the broken tarmac. One of the 'leutnants' was driving and Jack was squeezed in between the Colonel and the Major on the back seat. As the car bumbled fairly slowly along the road the occupants kept themselves awake by bellowing out various German marching songs. Jack tried ineffectually to join in but had to content himself with simply humming the tune.

After a further half-hour or so, the occupants of the car quietened down. The car was still travelling slowly but by now being steered more accurately. Signs of the army they were approaching began to appear on and around the road. Following Jack's suggestion the car was stopped to allow him to move into the front seat. Only a few minutes later they were stopped by a British sentry. Jack took a deep breath, hoping to hide the alcohol fumes, then hopped out and addressed the sentry, leaving the German officers in the car.

"These are my prisoners," he said. I have recovered the vehicle and I will be escorting them to the PoW compound."

"Very good Sar' Major," said the sentry. "Straight ahead sir."

Jack returned to the car, leaned in and suggested that the officers should remove their side-arms, which they did. He then changed places with the driver and drove the Mercedes in the direction indicated by the sentry, followed by the stares of the soldiers they passed. He stopped the car outside a wire fence leading away from each side of a hastily constructed tall wooden gate, switched off the engine and stepped out.

From the back seat of the car, the Colonel leaned out and thanked Jack for his help. "Now we must leave you and take the car inside," he said.

Jack stood by the open door of the car and smiled. "No sir," he said. It is me who will be taking the car while I am afraid you must take your belongings and walk to the gate. Please leave your pistols in the car."

The Colonel looked decidedly disgruntled for a moment then smiled and shrugged. "Ach zo," he said. "It is so." Then he clasped Jack by the hand and said "You are gut company, Oberfeldwebel"

The other three Germans climbed out of the car and all four of them marched to the gate in the wire, and into captivity.

* * * * * * * * * *

Jack came home just before Christmas in 1946. The Prisoner of War camps had been opened for the first time and groups of German prisoners in shabby worn-out clothing were shambling about the roads in the cold drizzly December day. Jack, his wife and young son were living with his mother and father and his two sisters in his parents' home. Although it was

57

a substantial house it was very cramped, however the occupants were looking forward to celebrating the first Christmas after the war as best they could.

Jack's mother kept chickens and one of her returning son's first duties had been to select and kill a suitable chicken for the family's Christmas dinner.

The house was decorated with home-made paper chains and some baubles. Jack's father had acquired a small tree by nefarious means and the family were about to sit down to Christmas Dinner.

Then Jack disappeared out through the front door. Five minutes later he came back, bringing with him five German prisoners of war. One was still dressed in the tattered remains of a Luftwaffe uniform. The Christmas Dinner was shared between thirteen rather than the eight for which it had been planned. Somehow it went round everyone and it became a joyous occasion.

The Political Interview

I was approaching retirement from my second career. For a long time I had been ignoring the inevitable advance of pensions and slippers by the fire, neither of which I was looking forward to. I had enjoyed a very busy life, travelling around the world, solving problems, creating more and dealing with the powerful and the trend-setters of every society.

I was having a quiet drink in the bar with my friend Robert and, inevitably, the conversation drifted around to my forthcoming retirement.

"You need a job," said Robert, placing his empty glass on the counter. I nodded. The barman dutifully refilled it with Club Claret.

"I've got a job, here," I said, somewhat unconvincingly.

"Yes," said Robert, picking up his glass. We sipped our wine in silence.

"Local government! That's the perfect thing for you. You'd be a whizz at it. Go for it. Go for county level, the rest isn't worth bothering about. I can tell you all about it if you like."

And that was how I found myself about to face the selection panel for the party candidate who would contest a local seat on the County Council, which was soon to become vacant.

The Party Agent had announced the opportunity of becoming a local politician several weeks ago. "Was I still interested?"

"Of course," I replied, which triggered a stream of instructions culminating in a statement that everything he had just told me would be confirmed by letter.

In due course the letter arrived and I seized the first opportunity to buttonhole Robert, who now held a very senior position in an adjacent County Council. "You'll walk it," he said. I looked unconvinced so he continued to boost my slightly flagging enthusiasm. "They are looking for people exactly like you," he continued. "They'll grab you with both hands."

Before the afternoon was over, Robert had written me a glowing testimonial which suggested that I could put the whole world to rights and with only a little more effort I could probably walk on water. The Club Chairman came in the next day and added an even more generous document, signing several copies in case they might be needed.

I wondered whether they were just keen to get rid of me but then decided that the thought was unworthy. Robert made a point of coming to my office several times to brief me on the curious world of the local politician. He followed this up with a couple of phone calls, by which time I felt myself ready to deal with even the most partisan and awkward questions from any interviewer.

I could not have been more wrong.

On the appointed day I cleared my desk early and with the 'good luck' wishes of my PA wringing in my ears I set off for the countryside after a light lunch. It took me a couple of hours to drive home and since the interview was scheduled for seven thirty that evening I was able to relax and even take the dog out for her evening walk before setting off for the interview. 'A cake-walk' I had been told.

The interview was to be held in the Parliamentary Constituency Headquarters situated in the tiny and ancient village of Marsden Seeland. It would start at seven-thirty sharp. There were to be four candidates and they were each expected to arrive by seven p.m. A strict timetable had been set out giving each candidate exactly forty minutes in front of the panel and I was the first candidate to be seen.

I asked the Constituency Agent to tell me who would be chairing the panel of selectors and how many interviewers there would be. There were no answers forthcoming to either of these questions.

I drove into the village square at about half past six, searched around with some difficulty until I found a space to park my car and then set off to locate the Constituency Headquarters. After several unsuccessful attempts asking passers-by if they knew where it was I started a process of elimination by trying the door handles on each of the buildings which looked as though they might have a political use.

Just before seven I tried the door handle on what looked like a redundant church. Bingo! This was it. As the door opened I found myself facing a four foot high poster bearing the current political slogan. The impact of the poster was somewhat damaged by the accumulation of grubby smears and dirty fingerprints which adorned it. It was further saddened by the tears and rips around the corners following multiple attempts to fix it to the cupboard door on which it now rested.

There were no lights on and the place exuded an uncared-for appearance through the darkening evening gloom. I threaded my way carefully past piles of printed 'flyers', sealed cardboard boxes, hessian sacks and a jumble of dusty books. There didn't seem to be anywhere to sit so I stood and waited. Seven o'clock came and went with nobody else appearing. At about ten minutes past the hour the front door opened and a nervous looking man wearing a moustache, a shock of ginger hair and a brown tweed suit peered in.

"Is this where the interviews are taking place?" He asked while a thin smile darted across his lower face, dying before reaching his eyes.

"I presume it is," I said. "I can't find anywhere else that looks likely so I suppose it must be."

"Right oh!"

"I can't find any chairs," I said, with a combined attempt at help and conversation.

"Not to worry, I'll sit on a box" he replied as he lowered himself gently onto a tower of two cardboard boxes. As his weight reached the first box it collapsed into the second one and my visitor collapsed majestically onto the floor. I helped him up and as he was dusting himself off the door opened and the third candidate joined us.

He was a younger man, smartly dressed in white shirt, blue tie and dark blue 'off-the-peg' suit.

I looked at my watch. It showed twenty-seven minutes past seven. I was wondering whether the whole thing was nothing more than a cruel hoax when another door, which I had not previously noticed, opened and a small scruffy looking man in a worn suit came in smiling and rubbing his hands together .

"Good, all here then, good," he said. "You'll be first then," he pointed at me. "There may be a bit of delay, you know how it is, shouldn't be long." He continued rubbing his hands together as he spoke. I wondered whether it might be appropriate to remind him that there were supposed to be four candidates but I dismissed the thought and decided to let him work it out for himself. "Just relax," he said, "I'll be back shortly" and he disappeared through the door from which he had recently emerged.

He left me feeling irritated. I had been told of the precise timing required and of the start time. I did not expect a delay at this point, I most certainly didn't know 'how it is' I had come a long way and was beginning to feel used, and finally I wondered where the fourth candidate was.

I made a conscious effort to put my irritation behind me and continued standing in the dim glow of a forty-watt bulb which had now been lit, joining my two companions in a game of avoiding eye contact.

I looked around the room. The forty-watt bulb had been a mistake because it merely served to show in greater detail just how cluttered, untidy and filthy the room really was.

The door opened and the slightly tousled head of my disorganised guide appeared in the gap. "Candidate number one" he intoned with unnecessary formality, or so I thought.

I followed the scruffy suit up a rickety and narrow stairway that looked as though it belonged in an England some time before the industrial revolution.

We reached the top of the stairs and stepped across two yards of dark corridor into a large cavernous room – 'a loft' I thought.

My guide announced my name, contradicting my assumption that he had forgotten it and he indicated an elderly frail-looking upright kitchen chair behind a small kitchen table. The table, I noticed seemed to house the entrances and exits of a substantial colony of woodworm.

I settled myself carefully into the chair, trying to remain prepared for it to collapse under me. It survived and I survived. I peered ahead into a room that seemed to be as dimly lit with as many dark corners as the one downstairs.

As my eyes became accustomed to the gloom I saw with amazement that the room around me was packed with people. There must have been at least forty-five men and women crammed in the circumference of a rough circle around the edges of the room.

Facing me from the far side of the room was a large man sporting an even larger gut which was straining the buttons of a bright pink shirt, open at the neck and at the next two buttons below. He was leaning far back in his chair which produced the effect of shoving his voluminous stomach further forward so that it became his dominant feature.

After a few moments, he began. "Well we all know each other here" he boomed, in the sort of voice public school bullies might have used to summon their 'Fags'. I didn't know anyone there but I didn't think it worth mentioning.

The pink shirt shuffled in his chair and began to speak. "Charles can't be here so I shall start. Why do you want to become our candidate?"

I hadn't a clue who Charles might be and I didn't really care. "I have had two very successful careers and I think it is time I put something back…"

I did not get any further. A crackly female voice screeched out of the darkness to my right, "Do you hunt?" it squawked in a tone that could probably break doors, let alone windows.

"Well, no, I…"

"Do you hunt? shrieked the hidden crone, sounding like one of the opening actors discussing 'eye of newt' in 'Macbeth'.

This time I got my answer in quickly. "No I don't hunt but I have nothing against it." I shouted, louder than I had intended.

And so it went on, with one fatuous piece of nonsense after another being hurled at me from out of the darkness.

I was asked by somebody in the shadows on the far side of the room, whom I couldn't really see, to list the things that I thought ought to be done to improve the lot of the rural inhabitants of the county. It wasn't really put like that though. The disembodied voice was male I thought, then possibly not,

I started to list the subjects I had rehearsed - affordable housing, the rural economy, the state of the roads, stop the closure of post offices....

I didn't get any further. A haughty, braying voice cut across the room. "So you believe in propping up failing businesses with public money, do you?"

The source of this rather crass interruption came from a tall, languid young man in a white shirt, with a shock of jet black hair and a fashionable curling lock of it hanging over one eye. Probably a product of one of the less successful public schools, I thought. I attempted a reply.

"No, I don't" I said with as much patience as I could muster. "I believe that the postal system remains vitally important, particularly to the elderly and those who can't travel far..."

"Hah!" he shouted. "Where are you going to get the money to keep open all these silly little shops?"

"You don't have to keep them open," I replied evenly. "You can provide the service from the back of a van, a counter in the pub, or tack it on to almost anything that is providing a service, even in the church hall if you like..."

"Hah! You townies don't know what you're talking about. You come here with your airs and graces..."

I was getting pretty fed up with this nonsense. "'I've lived in this county for forty years. My family has been here since the year 1610. My great, great grandfather was married in this village..." I was interrupted once again, this time by a croaking, whiney voice from my immediate right. It came from a wizened little man out of my field of vision but seated quite close to the right hand side of my small table.

"What about refuse? You mentioned refuse" said the gnome, with a distinct sneer.

I started to give my views on the importance of refuse collection when he cut me off again.

"Yer got it wrong!" He cried triumphantly. "Refuse is not the responsibility of the County Council. It's done by the District Council. I'm on the District Council.

"Does that mean I can't have a view?"

"No, yer can't."

My mind was racing. I grabbed at the first thought. I knew that roads or "highways", as the officials liked to call them, were the responsibility of the County Council. I also had the Fire Service in reserve but as I started to speak, the female idiot in the hidden corner squawked again

"Do you hunt?" The screech was a bit like scraping a knife on glass. Fortunately somebody else was asking a question, about postal voting I think.

A few moments later the ridiculous tortuous charade was brought to an end by the stomach in the pink shirt, whom, I actually thought, had gone to sleep.

"Well," he said, easing himself forward in his chair, "Thank you, er, Mr er, yes thank you, time's up I'm afraid."

And that was that.

I passed the next candidate on the stairs as I was going down. I wished him luck, with more sincerity than he might have thought. I wanted nothing more to do with that bunch of ill-mannered morons, and if that was local politics, I could do without it. I found my car, carried out a fifteen point turn to reverse direction towards home and drove away.

I had just settled down with a Loch Fyne whisky when the telephone rang. It was a few minutes before nine o'clock and according to the programme I had been given, the third candidate should have been just coming to the end of his interrogation.

I picked up the phone and a fruity voice, which also gave the impression of having downed its first gin, started talking. He gave his name but I didn't really catch it. He was in full flow and there was no opportunity for interruption.

"Well' jolly good evening, eh? Thought I should let you know that we have selected Marjorie. All good candidates, you know. Got to choose the best, well there it is. Hope we can count on your support..."

Very gently, I put the phone down. The whole thing had been a fix, a travesty - a show of going through the motions. I had seen no sign of Marjorie, who, had she been present among the candidates, would have been instantly noticeable because presumably she was a woman. Interestingly, I noted that the selection announcement had apparently been made five minutes before Marjorie was due to appear before the selection panel. They could not have spent much time discussing the candidates!

A few days later, when I was back in my office, I realised what a narrow escape I had had. If I had been successful I would have been communing with a bunch of county Neanderthals day and night, and, heaven forbid, even having to socialise with them. I felt I was a very lucky man.

The King of Spain's Father

It was a quiet afternoon when the phone on my desk rang. It was Simon, one of the First Sea Lord's Assistant Secretaries.

"The Sea Lord would like a word," he said.

"What about? Any idea?"

"None at all, I'm afraid. You know he doesn't confide in the lower orders who do all the work"

"O.K. I'm on my way" I said.

I climbed into my jacket and sauntered off along the sixth floor corridor of the Ministry of Defence. As I walked, I pondered on what type of crackpot scheme the great man might now have dreamed up to torment me with.

Thirty seconds later I walked into the Admiral's Secretary's office which was shared with the First Sea Lord's Naval Assistant.

"Go right in," said Charles, the long suffering but charming Captain who did service as secretary to the senior sailor. He had served in the capacity of secretary to this particular master for nearly twenty years. Occasionally, in a quiet pub, he would say to me "I often wonder why I stayed. The man is a self-serving gold plated bastard." This was how he would usually sum up his relationship with the most powerful man in naval uniform.

I knocked politely, waited a moment while there was, as usual, no response, then opened the door and strolled into the imposing room.

The First Sea Lord's office was a huge square room with a line of windows to the left of the entrance, which provided a view over Horseguards Avenue six floors below. On the far side of the room, diagonally opposite the door, the Admiral was seated on a comfortable upright chair behind a small desk. The corner to the left of the entrance was occupied by a group of four white leather armchairs surrounding a substantial circular coffee table. The remaining side of the room, immediately in front of the entrance was given over to a long, polished rectangular mahogany table surrounded by no less than fourteen matching chairs. By any standards the room was pretty big and it was known to make some visitors extremely nervous.

I pasted a smile on my face and strode confidently across the thick carpet to stand in front of the desk. "You wanted to see me, sir?" I said. He looked up, made a point of taking off his reading glasses and peered up at me. He did not suggest I should sit on the chair on the 'visitor's side' of the desk. It was to be a short interview.

After a moment he said "Ah, Tony, we're going to promote the King of Spain's father"

I waited. There would be more and I felt he was a little disappointed that I had not looked surprised at the strange announcement. 'Score one to me' I thought.

Easing back in his chair and toying with his fountain pen the great man continued. "It was the Prince of Wales's idea," he said.

I avoided the temptation to look baffled and waited for the next pearl of wisdom. It was not long in coming.

"You know that the King's father served in the Royal Navy?"

I didn't, but I replied, "oh yes sir." That seemed to be the right answer, so he continued with his idea of a briefing.

"The Prince has been on holiday with the King, you know." I nodded and he continued, "The old boy is actually an

69

Honorary Lieutenant in the Royal Navy and they thought that rank a bit lowly for the father of the King so the Prince had a word with me and I said we would arrange a ceremony to promote him to Honorary Admiral. What do you think?".

"An excellent idea," I said, knowing what would be coming next.

"Yes, so what I want you to do is to set it all up please. The Second Sea Lord can do the ceremony." He was already making squiggly notes on the edge of a document marked 'Top Secret'. The interview was over.

I deduced from the last mangled statement that the King's father, rather than the King, or the Prince of Wales, was to be promoted in one step across six levels of rank and that since the First Sea Lord no longer wished to bother with such trivia, the whole thing would be carried out by the Second Sea Lord, guided by me. I would now have to set up the whole project, liaising with 'our man in Spain', with the Spanish Embassy, the Second Sea Lord and his staff, the Foreign Office, the College of Arms and all sorts of other people. Until half an hour before I had never even heard of the King's father.

Over the next three months I found the King of Spain's father occupying more and more of my time. Every decision and every arrangement, no matter how trivial, had to be debated and changed time and again. It seemed that the Spanish authorities were going out of their way to be deliberately awkward and unco-operative.

One of the first tasks that came my way was to arrange for a vellum scroll to be produced as a sort of certificate to mark the event. I contacted the College of Arms and began an unproductive and difficult series of negotiations with a selection of the grandees who comprised the College. They were all absolutely charming, and they each sounded as though they were being so helpful – without actually being any help at all. First it was the timescale. Did I not realise that such documents were carefully drawn and painted by hand? Surely I was aware of the considerable workload already piling up for the draughtsmen of the College? Why had the 'Navy' not consulted the College before setting the timescale? And so it went on. Eventually, by bandying about names, from the Prince of Wales downward, I was able to extract an undertaking that the scroll would be completed and passed to me in exactly four months This would be two weeks before the event was to take place and it seemed to me to be cutting things fine. However it was the best I could do. The actual wording of the scroll, I was pleased to note, was regarded as being far too important to be left to me, and it would be drafted from a much higher pay grade. I was delighted.

The Second Sea Lord had got the bit between his teeth and numerous meetings were taking place inside his private office where orders of ceremony, food and wine to be served, table plans, guest lists and so forth were thrashed out, changed completely and thrashed out again. I had a strong feeling that most of these details were going to be dictated by the Spaniards but I thought it best not to mention that at this stage.

The Second Sea Lord rather fancied himself as a very special individual, with some justification I supposed, and so we who attended these meetings spent a lot of time listening to his stage directions governing how, where, and when the King's father would receive his promotion. These proceedings were reaching a crescendo when the bombshell arrived. I received a signal from the British Naval Attache in Madrid announcing that the King of Spain's father was not going to suffer the indignity and insult of being promoted by a mere

71

Second Sea Lord. It was to be the First Sea Lord, or the whole thing was off.

The Second Sea Lord was mortified, and he went into a sulk. It was rumoured that his wife had bought a whole new outfit for the event. The Second Sea Lord was a difficult man at the best of times; now he became a permanent grouch and most people within the Ministry tried to keep away from him.

I went off to find out how the First Sea Lord was taking the news. I was surprised to find that he was really quite chipper about it.

"I knew that they would need me," he confided one day as we sat in the back of his official car. "It's about Gibraltar, you know. I am the one person who can settle the Gibraltar problem."

There was no real answer to that so I just said "I see, sir." He seemed content with that and as we continued the journey he seemed distracted. I think, in his mind, he had just become the saviour of Gibraltar.

Shortly after this I was called to the First Sea Lord's office. This time I was invited to sit in the upright chair which was always placed close up to the desk at an angle of ninety degrees to the desk, so that the occupant would either have to listen to the Admiral's voice directed into his left ear or crane his neck around uncomfortably to look at the man on the other side of the desk.

I remembered, for a moment, the happy days when the Sir John, now Lord, Fieldhouse, had been the leader of the navy and our discussions had taken place in shirtsleeves, in the comfort of the white leather armchairs on the other side of the room, while I picked up the chair, placed it pointing towards the desk and sat in it.

"I've been thinking of what we should do to make this occasion special for the old man," said the Admiral.

I nodded, waiting for the gem that was about to emerge.

He leaned forward, elbows on his desk and hands forming a steeple while he smiled conspiratorially. "What we'll do," he said, "is dig out all of his confidential reports from when he was in the Royal Navy."

I began to feel, and, I suppose, look, worried. "Do you think that is a good idea, sir?" I asked as reasonably as I could. As I spoke I was also wondering where on earth these reports could be found, after all, we were talking about a period nearly fifty years ago and on the other side of both the Spanish Civil War and the Second World War. I was also uncomfortable about what might be contained within these reports. It was well known that senior officers, particularly at a time when captains felt more powerful and unfettered, that confidential reports were frequently used as vehicles for unsubtle wit, castigation or even revenge, to the detriment of the unfortunate subject of the report.

"Do you think that's a good idea sir?" I ventured very carefully.

"Yerrs, chaps love to see things like that." He was now smiling and I wondered why.

"Well, they may be difficult to get hold of and they might include some criticism or 'adverse comments'..." I tailed off with the formal pair of words which could mean the most damning remarks that might even spell the end of an officer's career.

"No problem getting hold of them. They'll be in the Records Office at Kew. Just need to pop along there and get some copies. Do you know which ships he served in?" he asked, suddenly changing the direction of the discussion. I had

73

learnt that this was his way of bringing any debate to an end, and was really a polite form of "...just do it my way or else..."

There was really nothing more to say so I took my leave, went back along the sixth floor corridor to my office and suggested to my assistant that he might like to drive down to Kew, locate the reports, if he could, and bring back copies. He was a young man who found life among the Ministers and Mandarins boring , so he was off like a shot.

It was late in the afternoon before I was able to see the early naval reports on the Count of Barcelona, as the King's father was known. There were five reports written by the captains of the five battleships that Don Juan Carlos had served in after he had graduated from Britannia Royal Naval College at Dartmouth, qualifying in Navigation and Gunnery.

The first thing that began to bother me was why had Don Juan Carlos served in so many different ships? He had spent less than three years in the seagoing navy and usually, in such a short period an officer would serve in only one ship, perhaps two at the most. I was looking at five reports, and none of them seemed encouraging.

The first report was blunt indeed. It said "I want this officer out of my ship. He is a bad influence on the men. His view of the Royal Navy is that it provides a ready source of rum, brandy, gin, whisky and cheap cigarettes, nothing more."

The second report wasn't much better, although it did explain in more detail why the report's author had taken such a dislike to his young Spanish Lieutenant.

"This officer seems to believe that life in the Royal Navy should consist entirely of Pimms parties and the like. He drinks far too much gin for his own good – and for that matter brandy, port and rum. He has been reprimanded for smoking near the Cordite Magazine. He takes little notice of orders given and I cannot manage him with such an attitude."

The third report went on about joining the sailors for their daily issue of rum, leading them astray on runs ashore, and preventing the application of what was described as 'proper discipline'. As I read on I was beginning to warm to Don Juan Carlos. Clearly he had been a bit of a hell-raiser, an inspiring leader of 'runs ashore' warmly regarded by the ratings and a thorn in the side of the rather pompous command structure of the nineteen thirties. By the time I had read the fourth and fifth reports I believed that he had been an all-round good egg, the life and soul of any party and a friend to a sailor in need. He didn't give a hoot for any potential career in the Royal Navy – why should he? He was adept, as one senior officer's handwritten note added "at treading the fine line between discipline and insubordination, just on the wrong side of it." His happy-go-lucky, devil-may-care attitude had got right up the noses of authority and as a result he had been moved on from ship to ship as soon as possible – rather like a grand round of 'Pass the Parcel'.

I had never met him but I liked him already. Every organization, I thought, needs somebody like the Count. In fact when I met him later, I found he was a man of immense charm with a considerable sense of fun which was undiminished by advancing age and illness.

I typed up the five reports onto a single sheet of paper, phoned the P.A. to check that my master was available, and strolled off along the corridor towards the First Sea Lord's suite of offices. As I approached the corner of the corridor I noticed a group of earnest looking men in animated conversation with one of the Ministers. I didn't recognise any of them so I presumed they were the latest intake of aspiring

Mandarins. Such last minute discussions were not uncommon in the corridors of the Ministry so I took little notice. The group broke up as I approached, the Minister turned towards the shelter of his office and the other three turned the corner, gaining distance on me since they were walking rather faster. As I followed them around the corner I spotted two or three sheets of A4 paper, clipped together and lying on the tiles in the centre of the corridor. The top sheet was stamped, unmistakably, in red. 'TOP SECRET' it said. I stood by the paper and called to the three figures, now ten yards in front of me.

"Excuse me!" I yelled. There was no response, so I repeated my call even louder. This time they stopped and one, clutching a bundle of files, turned an irritable face towards me.

I pointed at the floor. "Did you drop this?" I called.

There was no answer but the man with the files scurried back along the corridor, looked at me distastefully, leaned down to scoop up the paper – and dropped the rest of his bundle of files. He didn't speak. In particular, he didn't thank me, so I walked around the untidy heap of important papers and continued towards the Sea Lord's office.

I had to wait a few moments so I stood chatting to the Admiral's Secretary until the door opened to discharge the visitor. I grabbed the door before it closed, pasted a smile on my face, and breezed in. "I have those confidential reports, sir," I said.

I handed over my sheet of paper and stood by the desk, waiting. A frown came over the First Sea Lord's face while he peered at the paper. He put it down then picked it up again, put on his reading glasses and scrutinised the five short reports once more.

At length he looked up. "Whose idea was this?" He demanded.

I was ready for this. This man did not wish to be associated with mistaken assumptions or failed plans. "I am afraid I really can't remember," I said, adding "But I would like you to know that it was not mine."

He harrumphed. A small pyrrhic victory to me, I thought. I turned away because my boss was already busying himself once more with the pile of documents on the blotter in front of him.

When I returned to my office another significant problem awaited me. A stack of signals was sitting on my desk. The Admiralty Board had already decided that a modern British frigate should be sent to Spain to provide the venue for the ceremony. The Spaniards had responded by detailing two of their frigates and announcing that the event would take place in the Spanish port of Cartagena on the Mediterranean coast. The Spaniards were providing a naval band and I had arranged for a Royal Marines Band to attend. I had also arranged for a C130 Hercules aircraft of the Royal Air Force to transport the Royal Marines Band to the airport at Murcia, about seventy miles north east of Cartagena.

The Spanish authorities had just announced that the Royal Marines would not be allowed to play and march on Spanish territory, namely on the jetty alongside the ship. They were incensed by the fact that the Royal Marines wear a cap badge with a small image of Gibraltar superimposed on it. There was talk of calling off the whole project, which would inevitably result in a marked display of huffiness by the Spaniards. There were more arguments about which of the three ships would be used for the ceremony but I felt we would be able to dust off that ploy. We had just six weeks to go.

A few days later, another meeting took place with the First Sea Lord. The confidential report scheme had been abandoned and he had now come up with another idea.

"What we can do," he said, "is get a small piece of Victory oak and have it carved into a stud box, or something like that."

"The Spaniards are already a bit tetchy," I said, "and they might remember that HMS Victory was not on their side."

He gave me a withering look and ignored my comment. "The C.O. of Victory is going to phone you."

I went back to my office and within a couple of hours the phone call arrived. The Commanding Officer of HMS Victory explained that he had one expert who would be able to take and carve a small piece of Victory oak – allegedly a piece of oak that once formed part of Britain's most famous sailing battleship. I was told that it would take the carver about three weeks to complete the work. That would be just two weeks before the ceremony was to take place. I went home relatively happy.

A week later the finger of fate struck again – twice! The first thing to dent my good humour was the arrival of the illuminated scroll from the Royal College of Arms. It arrived heavily wrapped in a strong cardboard tube. I put it away in my safe but then, as the day wore on I began to worry about whether it was alright. Before I left the office that evening I took the package out of the safe, stripped off the packaging and carefully withdrew the rolled vellum scroll. I spread it out on my desk and marvelled at it. It was a truly magnificent work of art, with superb copper-plate writing and brilliant heraldic colours.

Then as I stared at the beautiful document I froze. There was a spelling mistake! I couldn't believe it! Surely not.

I checked and, without doubt, it was there. The document was headed with the name of the recipient. It should have read 'Don Juan Carlos y Bourbon y Battenberg'. In this one 'Battenberg' was spelt '*Batenberg*'. I put the document back in its protective tube and popped it in one of the big locked cupboards. It no longer justified the security of my safe. I drove home that evening, unable to dismiss the thought that the College of Arms had insisted on nearly two months to prepare the important document, stressing the lengthy time it took to draw and paint such a document entirely by hand.

Early next morning I telephoned the College of Arms and informed them of the problem. The very important chap that took my call refused, at first, to believe that there really was a mistake, then changed tack to assert that the College could not possibly have originated the mistake. I told him that I was merely the messenger and the whole thing had been handled by the office of the First Sea Lord. I added that they always kept authenticated copies of such documents. The voice on the other end of the line began to change and take on a more apologetic and placatory tone.

When I put down the phone I trotted along to the Secretary to the First Sea Lord, gave him a synopsis of my telephone discussion, presented him with the damning evidence of the scroll and made myself scarce very quickly. I had no wish to be present when the bad news was conveyed to my master.

I had only been back in my own office for twenty minutes when fate struck again. The phone rang. My assistant answered it and then wordlessly handed it to me. I listened to an anguished foreman from Portsmouth Dockyard explaining to me that the only man capable of carving the required oaken stud box had been riding his bike through the dockyard when disaster had overtaken him. He had managed to get the front wheel of his bike stuck in the railway lines that run all over the dockyard and had been pitched over the handlebars. He had broken his right arm and would not be capable of carving anything for a long time to come.

I interrupted the story and cheerfully told the foreman that the First Sea Lord would expect him to find another carver to finish the job. I said "goodbye" and put the phone down before he had an opportunity to protest. We had less than two weeks to go.

Later that day the Royal Marines, never ones to be deflected from their aim, came up with a novel solution to the refusal of the Spaniards to allow them to play on Spanish soil.

****

Miraculously, eleven days later, the First Sea Lord, his wife, his Naval Assistant, his Chief Steward and I climbed into two smart black cars outside his flat in Admiralty Arch and set off for Heathrow. It was just before seven in the morning and the traffic was mercifully light. In my briefcase I had a replacement scroll and an exquisitely carved oak stud box. I had kept well clear of the details concerning the frantic rate of production of both items.

We drove in convoy through a back gate on the far side of the airfield and shortly after seven thirty I was climbing up the aircraft-mounted boarding steps into an HS 125 of the Queen's Flight. The aircraft was already moving before the door was pulled up behind me, and we didn't stop moving till we reached the threshold of the runway. A few minutes later we were climbing steeply away from Heathrow, just entering the first layer of cloud.

As we crossed the channel, the cloud beneath us cleared away and we cruised along under a brilliant, clear blue sky.

We crossed the Pyrenees, being given a superb view of the mountain range in all its glory. Ten minutes or so after that we began to let down for the approach to the joint military and commercial airport at Murcia.

The layout inside the small executive jet was quite unlike the usual aircraft seating pattern. There was a plush three seater sofa along the starboard side of the cabin while the rest of the space was occupied by a series of comfortable, compact armchairs, some of them being mounted on swivels, which could be locked for take-off and landing.

As we turned in a gentle descending turn to line up with the runway I could see that we had the airspace over the airfield entirely to ourselves. The single pilot called "finals" and began the final approach to land. During the trip, two flight attendants had kept up a supply of coffee, tea, delicate sandwiches and other refreshments so everyone was in a fairly mellow, relaxed mood as we approached the runway. I noted that the First Sea Lord was sitting beside his wife on the sofa, with a file of papers on his lap. He was just going over the speech he expected to make when we arrived onboard our frigate in Cartagena.

Suddenly our world was almost literally turned upside down. The aircraft banked violently to starboard with full power applied to both engines. Instinctively I looked towards the row of small round windows on my left, to see what was causing our pilot to take such radical avoiding action. What I saw shocked me. I could see a red painted right-hand wing tip just outside the nearest window. I could also see a similarly painted left-hand wing tip just outside the forward-most window on my left. The cabin momentarily darkened as the other aircraft, which seemed to be wearing the colours of a trainer, zoomed close past and above the left side of our aircraft.

Inside the cabin, all was now chaos. The First Sea Lord's wife was lying on the cabin floor screaming hysterically, the Admiral's papers were still flying around among the seats. The RAF attendant had fallen, spraying a tray of teacups and plates over everyone and everything.

I had been strapped into my seat near the back of the cabin and I had avoided the worst of the disaster. I unstrapped and tried to help some of the others to recover the situation, while the aircraft continued in a wide circle, returning to the point of the incident.

This time we landed without further incident. Composure was recovered while we taxied in to a wide concrete dispersal area, on the other side of which stood a long line of Mercedes limousines and Spanish Guardia Civil cars, blue lights flashing impressively.

I spoke briefly to our white faced, white knuckled pilot and confirmed what I had seen. He was pleased to get this piece of evidence from a fellow aviator and he marched off purposely in the direction of the control tower.

We had been unashamedly 'buzzed' at very close quarters by another aircraft and my view was that, with an otherwise empty airfield, this could not have been an accident. However by the time I reached the reception party and the line of cars I discovered that the twenty or so drivers and others all swore that they had seen no other aircraft. Later, I learned that our pilot was getting the same story from the occupants of the Control Tower. It might have seemed clever to put us off our stroke but it was thoroughly dangerous and unacceptable.

We piled into the various cars with members of the reception team and set off in a tightly packed convoy, heading for Cartagena, seventy miles away. The convoy was led by a Guardia Civil car with another police car interspersed between each of the limousines and at the end of the line.

The convoy wound up to at least seventy miles per hour and hurtled along the highway. Every time we passed through or near a village or small town I noticed that the whole place was sealed off with what seemed like a complete battalion of the quasi-military police.

In less than an hour we were travelling, rather more slowly, through the town of Cartagena, heading towards the Naval Dockyard.

We had planned to stop our car just inside the dockyard gates so the First Sea Lord's flag could be mounted on the front of the car. Our leader was unaware of this plan, and when, just outside the dockyard, he realised that the flag was not flying, he shouted. "My flag! Stop!"

Dutifully, the driver slammed on the brakes. The driver of the police car behind was taken by surprise and his car ran with an expensive-sounding crunch into the back of our car. The flag was quickly set in place on the bonnet while the two drivers stared at the damage to both cars. We limped on in the direction of HMS Beaver, our frigate, which was identified by the sound of a piper from the Scots Guards performing on the jetty, by the foot of the gangway.

****

The rest of that day went surprisingly smoothly. We met the British Ambassador as we arrived at the ship. As we waited for everyone to emerge from the cars Lady Gordon-Lennox, the wife of the Ambassador sought a little advice from me on a matter of protocol.

"I believe Lady Staveley is called Bettina," she said. "Should I call her Betty?"

"Only once," I replied.

The British Ambassador and the First Sea Lord led the way up the brow to the frigate's immaculate flight deck and were duly 'piped' aboard. They were followed by their spouses and the rest of us. As we moved towards the ship's brow the Spanish band struck up a slightly discordant military tune which for some reason reminded me of the background music to the film of John Wayne defending the Alamo. It didn't last long though. The music from the jetty was suddenly drowned by a stirring rendering of "Hearts of Oak", played with the skill and gusto that only the 'Royals' can muster. The Spanish band played on, marching up and down the dockside but nobody could hear them from the ship so nobody took any notice. The Royal Marines band was actually spread out all over the superstructure of the ship, from which position their music was predominant.

Then I noticed that the frigate's large flight deck was covered with a rather fine fitted blue carpet. At the far end of the deck a dais and lectern had been set up, complete with a microphone system. A lot of important looking people were milling about in front of several rows of chairs, placed in the hangar facing the dais.

Before the main event took place the guests were invited to tour the upper deck of the ship and while we did so we were treated to an impressive close quarters flying display by the frigate's two Lynx helicopters. Afterwards everyone was shepherded back to the seats in the hangar. So far, I couldn't discern any input from the two smart Spanish frigates, apart from being present and sending their captains to the ceremony.

The Lynx helicopters disappeared, the bands ceased their musical battle and the First Sea Lord climbed onto the dais. The Admiral was very good at this sort of thing and this occasion was to be no exception. He started to speak from a script but soon moved away from this to talk in informal – but very carefully rehearsed – terms of the historic links between the two countries, the honour bestowed on the Royal Navy by having enjoyed Don Juan Carlos's service as a sea-officer, what an inspiration he had been and what a fine fellow he was. He didn't mention the Armada, the destruction of the Spanish fleet at Trafalgar, or Gibraltar. Images of hundreds of years of jolly tars hammering the 'Dons' flitted through my mind.

The scroll and the small package containing the Victory oak stud box were presented and hands were warmly shaken, complete with elbow clutching, all to the roar of tumultuous applause.

Then it was the turn of Don Juan Carlos himself. He climbed onto the dais and started to speak in a gravelly voice, the product of his illness, in almost unaccented English. He smiled as he recounted his fond memories of the Royal Navy. "Plenty of gin," he said, "plenty of brandy, rum, whisky, port, Madeira, good wines and all the cigars and cigarettes one could smoke." He rolled on, "no real responsibilities," he said, "a few difficult people about, but not many..." I wondered whether the same recollections of the rather damning confidential reports were running through my Admiral's mind as were crowding into my own.

The speech ended to another enthusiastic round of applause, the Royal Marines band struck up a rousing tune – just managing to drown out the Spanish band which was attempting to start playing once again on the dockside, and we all trundled in to lunch. The lunch party consisted of the Admiral and our group from London, a selection of ship's officers, the captains of the adjacent Spanish ships and some senior Spanish officers. The remainder consisted of friends of Don Juan Carlos, all of whom seemed to be dukes, counts, princes or other grandees.

I found myself seated beside the current Duke of Medina Sidonia, so inevitably, we started discussing the Spanish Armada. The Duke was a very engaging and polished, youngish man with an interest in international yacht racing and sufficient means to ensure that he would never have to use the word 'overdraft'.

Lunch itself was superb. I learnt that the menu had been stipulated by the Casa Real – the Royal House – but cooked by the ship's chefs. Each of the five courses was accompanied by a different and excellent Spanish wine, in addition to a small glass of neat spirit. We started with sherry, to accompany the soup, then followed with gin, rum, brandy, whisky liqueur and finally several glasses of vintage port. Additionally, before we sat down we were invited to have a couple of glasses of champagne. Quite a few of the guests were smoking before and during the courses so the gaps in the partially open hangar doors were useful.

Eventually, hands were shaken, promises made to meet again and we all took our leave. The Royal Marines reached the end of their concert, leaving the Spanish band, still struggling on the jetty, to be heard at last. We climbed aboard the cars and, with the Royal Marines bugle salute still ringing in our ears, we drove away, somewhat more slowly and with a smaller Guardia Civil escort this time, heading for the airport.

The First Sea Lord confided in the other two passengers that, with the British Ambassador he was to have dinner that evening in Madrid with senior Spanish naval officers and some politicians. We, his staff were to check in to one of Madrid's finest hotels and then we would be free to amuse ourselves for the rest of the evening – while he was confident, he said, that he would solve the Gibraltar problem once and for all. I wondered if he would last the evening after all that food and booze at lunch.

We hangers-on enjoyed a good, if light, dinner, visited a flamenco show and wandered back, tired but happy. Next morning we arrived at the airport before the First Sea Lord. He turned up about twenty minutes after we should have taken off, looking distinctly glum. Someone ventured to ask whether he had actually managed to resolve the Gibraltar problem, and received a scathing look and a snapped reply for their trouble. It seemed the great man had failed in his quest and was feeling the results of his excesses of the previous day.

We flew back in silence to Heathrow, maintained most of the silence in the car which took us to the Ministry of Defence and then wandered off to our respective offices. Don Juan Carlos, Count of Barcelona was now an Honorary Admiral in the Royal Navy and we were all free to forget it and get on with whatever was coming next.

The Secretary From Hell

The recruitment process had taken a very long time and, so far as I could tell, it had been conducted very carefully. I had made it clear that I wanted someone quite different from the previous occupant of the swivel chair. I didn't want to be saddled with a dolly bird – all high heels and painted nails, I had said. No, I was looking for a well-qualified mature lady who would be capable with a typewriter and even more capable with a computer, who would have an excellent telephone manner, and be thoroughly reliable. She would need to be able to take fast and accurate shorthand and to manage the set-up and support of the numerous committee meetings I was saddled with.

The selection panel had looked at the offerings of about six West-End agencies and had conducted preliminary interviews with at least twenty candidates. This seemed to take an inordinate amount of time but at last, I was told that there were now just four candidates, all of whom I was invited to meet and have an informal chat with, before the final selection was made by the panel – chaired by my remarkable lady Financial Controller who had the ability to put the fear of God into any other staff member, including managers, just by a twitched eyebrow followed by a silent, penetrating stare.

The four aspiring secretaries were wheeled into my office one at a time during the course of a single afternoon and over cups of tea I chatted with them, trying to gauge their personalities and to see whether they would fit in to the curious world of clubland. They all seemed to be able to meet the requirements of the job but for some reason that I couldn't really pin down, I could not seem to take to the third of the four ladies. I dutifully passed on this rather vague view and so, about a week later the final three were invited back to the club, given formal interviews by the panel, tested in shorthand and computer skills, taken to meet key members of the staff such as the chef and then sent on their way while the panel deliberated on their preferred choice.

Later, much later, that evening, the chairman of the panel came to my office and informed me that the unanimous choice to be my secretary would be a lady who went by the name of Elizabeth. I was given a file stuffed with references and other papers and invited to contact no less than five referees myself. She came, I was told, with the very highest recommendations of the recruitment agency, having passed, with flying colours, every test the agency could devise. She was to start work a few days before the Christmas closure but for the first two weeks she would be employed as a "Temp" still on the books of the agency. This, I supposed, would be a combined induction and probationary period.

I started into the list of referees with enthusiasm, anxious to fill the empty chair in the outer office as soon as I could. I telephoned the first referee on the list, apologised for disturbing him so late in the evening and asked him if he would be prepared to give me a view on the skills and suitability of Elizabeth for the many sided role I was offering. The response was encouraging. This man had not worked directly with Elizabeth but he had been a director of the company where she had been employed as a Personal Assistant to one of his colleagues. He said she seemed competent, industrious and a reliable team member. I thanked him and moved on to the next one. This was a titled lady who had chaired a charitable committee and who remembered Elizabeth as a useful supporting member of her team. I was left with the impression that she didn't actually know Elizabeth particularly well but she had no criticism to offer. It seemed that Elizabeth had adopted the role of reliable "worker bee", not outstanding but always willing to take the minutes, type the agendas, make the tea and do the washing up.

The next two referees told similar stories although on the whole, their knowledge of Elizabeth was related to a period some time in the past. In one case the interaction had been in an unpaid social environment but in the other case it was set in a professional role however the referee seemed a bit vague.

I rang the final referee a couple of times. There was no answer on the first occasion and on the second occasion, after listening for a considerable period, to the ringing at the other end of the line, I was treated to a short chorus of clicks and rattles before being invited to leave my name and number. I left my contact details and silently convinced myself that four out of five at the first try, was not bad going and despite little of the information being current I had not heard any criticism of the lady. Additionally my selection team had carried out a detailed assessment of personality and character as well as setting a number of professional tests, all of which had been satisfactorily accomplished.

As I strolled through the club on my way to my car I could not shake off a strange feeling of doubt and concern regarding Ms Elizabeth. I dismissed the thought as being unworthy and drove home. By the time I had spent an hour negotiating London's late evening traffic I had forgotten my reservations. I arrived home to a cheerful greeting from my wife, a mouth-watering aroma of grilling steak emerging from the kitchen and the usual enthusiastic welcome from Cassie and Bruen, our pair of golden retrievers. My secretarial recruitment task disappeared completely from my thoughts.

* * * * * * * * * *

A watery sun was trying to brighten the London street scene as my car emerged from the tunnel into Piccadilly and came to a stop among three lanes of stationary traffic. The next task before me, as every morning, was to negotiate myself across the slow moving traffic so that I could turn through the tall iron gates into the front courtyard. I parked the car, picked up my briefcase and strolled through the club towards my office, answering the cheery greetings of my staff as I strolled along. Almost as soon as I walked into the outer office I was told that my new secretary would be arriving this very morning. It was then about half past eight so I assumed, as I prowled through my in-tray that I would be meeting her within half an hour.

The half hour went by, followed by another, then another. I wasn't concerned and I imagined that the lady was probably completing her joining routine somewhere else in the building. It therefore came as something of a surprise when the outer door banged open and a large woman laden with an assortment of shopping bags and parcels clattered in and stood outside my open office door.

She peered in through the open doorway. "Are you the Club Secretary?"

"Er, yes," I said, somewhat surprised.

"Where's my desk then?"

A tiny frisson of doubt was creeping towards my brain. "Jackie will show you around," I called, then, "Come in as soon as you've settled in. I have some letters to dictate." I had six letters requiring answers so I placed them in a small pile on one side of the desk while I busied myself with an examination of the Daily Telegraph. I became distantly aware of the noises of moving furniture accompanied by other thumps and bumps from the outer office so, after ten minutes or so, I decided to do a tour of my domain and make sure that all was well with the Club. As I strode out into the Reception Hall, I averted my eyes from the jumbled disarray of desk, table and chairs which had been previously the location of my Secretary. On the far side of the big communal office, Jackie, usually phlegmatic and undemanding, was standing, hands on hips, glaring at the growing disruption with a look of shock on her face.

I strolled off to visit Heinrich in his busy kitchen, walked through to the front hall, took a glance outside, pointed out some litter which had blown in and then made my way back, via the Member's Bar and the Smoking Room, to my offices.

I walked in, smiled at Ms Elizabeth and asked her to come in to my small office, and bring her notebook. She followed me in and parked her ample frame in one of the three spare upright chairs. She sat and looked at me expectantly, pencil in one hand and notebook in the other.

I started with the usual pleasantries, welcomed her to the Club and hoped she would quickly settle in and enjoy the work. I didn't need to ask about her background or previous experience because I had already read all about it – or so I thought.

She wasn't very forthcoming and didn't have much to say so I got on with the dictation. There was no answering smile. She got up and strode out to her desk in the outer office. I followed her out and set off once more to continue my rounds of the building. I took my time and so it was at least two hours later when I returned to the office. Ms Elizabeth didn't seem to be doing much typing so I decided she must have finished the work.

In fact I was due to attend an informal meeting of the Ball Committee which had already started in one of the ornate banqueting rooms. I sat and listened to the proposals of the committee members, noting that some would have to be rejected, but not now. Now was the time for me to keep my powder dry.

Inevitably the meeting droned on into lunchtime and we all ended up in the Member's Bar. As soon as I could reasonably prize myself away I went off to Join John, my Deputy, for a light lunch in the Coffee Room.

When I arrived back in the office after lunch I was immediately struck by the rather frosty atmosphere that seemed to pervade the room. As I passed the desk of my new secretary I asked if the letters were ready.

"No" came the rather abrupt answer.

"Well just give me the ones you have done" I said, as reasonably as I could manage, while hiding my irritation.

"I haven't done any."

I was shocked. "Why not?" I demanded.

Ms Elizabeth looked up from the seat she was sprawled in and responded in a moaning, miserable tone, "the phone keeps ringing."

"Yes, it does that, that's what it's for." I said, beginning to show my exasperation. On the other side of the room I could almost feel the waves of embarrassment emerging from Jackie, who was trying to appear busy with some banqueting files.

"You haven't typed up any of those letters?" I asked for the second time.

"I've got a headache."

"Oh," I said, not very gently.

"...and I can't make that work." She jabbed a fat hand towards the desk top computer. "I think I'm getting a migraine." This statement was concluded with a sort of sob.

Things were at an impasse so I said, "well you had better go home then." She didn't need telling twice. With remarkable speed and agility she started gathering her things and was already on her feet ready to go while I still stood in front of her.

"I'm surprised you can't work the computer," I said, "but we can easily fix that. If you come in a bit earlier tomorrow morning I will arrange for someone to take you through the whole thing." She was already trying to edge round me, heading for the door.

"I'll see you at eight o'clock then," I said.

"Alright." And then she was gone!

The expert in secretarial technology in those days was Sharon. Additionally, Sharon, who was Membership Secretary, was always first to arrive in the morning which meant she would not be unduly disturbed at having to appear at eight o'clock.

I made a special effort and for once the stream of commuting traffic was co-operative. I drove into the front courtyard at seven forty-five but Sharon was already waiting for me in the office. We chatted over coffee while we waited for our pupil to arrive. At eight o'clock we were still waiting, and at eight-thirty, and at nine o'clock.

Feeling frustrated and not a little angry, I sent Sharon off to get on with her proper job just after nine.

The mail was delivered at half past nine and I went through it with the help of Jackie, just as we had been doing over the previous months. At ten o'clock I had a short meeting with a newly joined member and I was just saying goodbye to him when the slightly tousled shape of my new secretary, complete with her array of bags, shuffled past me into the office.

I shook hands with my new member and turned back into the office. The time was a few minutes after ten-thirty. "I see you weren't able to get in early this morning?" I said, trying to keep my voice even.

She yawned! She actually yawned! "No," she said, "I was *far* too tired this morning."

I am not usually lost for words but I was then so I simply walked away. I sat behind my desk, pondering, for a few moments then decided that I should get Sharon to carry out the required computer training while I gave the developing problem more thought. I shut the office door – a very unusual departure from my habitual 'open-door' policy and phoned Sharon to explain that her pupil had finally decided to put in an appearance. A couple of hours later I left for lunch, still pondering the problem.

On my way back to the office I popped downstairs to the Membership office to check that Sharon had successfully completed the short course of instruction. She was hesitant and careful with her response but did assure me that the computer operation had been fully explained and she had left it with the Word Processing programme on the screen, ready to accept typed input.

I strolled back up the stairs and into the office, pausing to ask my new secretary if she had finished any of the letters I had dictated on the previous day.

"No, not yet," she said, without looking up from her desk.

This was not the answer I expected. As I was forming my response I noticed that her desk was covered in Christmas cards and envelopes. I started to say that I thought all of the

95

Club Christmas cards had already been sent when I realised that the cards were not those of the Club. "What are those?" I asked.

"Oh, these are my Christmas cards," she said.

"Yours?"

"Yes, they're mine, but I'm a bit late in sending them." She was still busy scribbling signatures and placing cards in envelopes and had not yet looked up.

"What about my letters?" I said, beginning to show anger in my voice. On the other side of the room Jackie glanced up, sensing trouble.

"I'll get around to them."

"Why haven't you done them?" I demanded.

At last she looked up. "The phone keeps ringing," she said. Then as an afterthought she added "…and I'm getting a terrible headache. I think I've got a migraine coming on."

Jackie stopped typing and stared across the room in shock.

I realised that I had heard this response almost exactly 24 hours previously. Additionally, this woman had languished on the payroll for two days and had contributed precisely nothing to the benefit of the business. Something had to be done.

I dropped into my swivel chair and started rooting about in my overflowing in-tray, searching for the telephone number of the agency which had supplied the useless encumbrance, who had by now gathered up all her cards and bags and was passing my open doorway, heading home. Did I see a small smirk of satisfaction on her face?

I found the paper I was looking for and I reached towards the telephone. Before my hand touched it, it began to ring. I picked it up, paused for a moment to calm down then answered the call.

96

A pleasant, well-spoken and sonorous voice announced himself as the recent Chairman of a major national charity, and the former employer of my new secretary. What he had to say alarmed me and confirmed me in my decision.

"Don't touch that woman with a long pole!" He said. "She's poison – absolute poison!"

"She's already here," I responded rather weakly.

"You mean she's already working for you?" He sounded horrified.

"No," I said, "She has been here for two days but 'working' would be going too far."

"I understand you," he said, "but that's only the tip of the iceberg. She has a really violent temper and she will spring into a rage at the drop of a hat. Get rid of her." He said again.

I didn't really know how to reply so the line stayed silent for a few moments. Then he started again. "You know she's a member of the Tudor Society?"

"Yes," I said.

"Well, have a look at the 'London Diary' column in the 'Mail'. Go back a couple of weeks, maybe three and you will see that she stood up in a meeting at the Southwark Hall and threw a packet of ham sandwiches at the Chairman during his speech. A week later the paper printed an apologetic retraction. They said the sandwiches weren't ham, they were cheese! Point is, she certainly threw the food at a distinguished historian who had done nothing to offend her. She's an uncontrollable nut!" He paused, then added, more quietly "She's a bitch with a foul and unpredictable temper. For God's sake don't cross her."

I had heard enough. With what I had just been told and the experience of the last two days I wanted nothing more to do with Ms Elizabeth. Fortunately, in negotiating the recruitment and joining process we had agreed with the recruitment agency that Elizabeth would remain on the books of the agency for her first two weeks, working for us as a 'Temp'. This would cover the Christmas holiday period so she would then be enrolled as a Club employee early in the New Year. A small silent prayer accompanied a flood of relief as I picked up the phone and dialled the number for the secretarial agency. I asked to be put through to the lady in charge, who was in fact the owner.

* * * * * * * * * *

When she came on the line I didn't waste any time on niceties. I just said "I've had enough of Elizabeth. I don't want to see her any more. She has gone home with yet another headache, having achieved precisely nothing in the two days she has been here – so she's yours.

"I don't understand. We thought she would be perfect for the job – and she was so looking forward to it!"

"Well, I said, she has not appeared in the office before ten o'clock on either of the two days she has been here, she claims not to be able to understand the word processor and she has not done anything productive except write Christmas cards – her own Christmas cards, that is, and she has gone home each day after lunch with a headache. And the final straw is that I have just spoken to her principal referee who informs me that she has a foul and unpredictable temper. He recommends that I should get rid of her as soon as possible." I paused, and then finished more quietly with "I'm sorry to remind you that she is still on your books as a temp – and she is one temp whom I never wish to set eyes on again. Please get in touch with her and tell her not to come back."

There was a long pause, then the agency lady said again "I don't understand." There was a prolonged silence while she gathered her thoughts, then she continued "I just don't understand. She seemed so nice when she was here. She came through all of our tests with flying colours, her shorthand is fast and accurate and so is her typing..."

I interrupted, "but she has a personality that could kill bulls and burn paint! I'm sorry to be pedantic but she's yours. However I still need a secretary, can you give that some thought?"

"Yes, I'll do that, but first I'd better send for Elizabeth and give her the bad news. By the way, are you sure it's not just a personality clash? Did you actually give her any work to do?"

"Firstly, as far as I'm concerned there wasn't any opportunity to collide personalities either with me or anyone else. She wasn't here long enough. However she seems to have achieved a personality war with her previous boss. He was emphatic. Secondly, the answer is yes, I did give her work to do. I dictated six short letters two days ago and she hasn't even started the first digit of the first word of the first letter. I tell you, she is less use than an empty chair." I drew a breath and added "And an empty chair isn't likely to bite!"

"OK. I'll call her in and I'll get back to you. But there must be some misunderstanding."

I put the phone down, sat for a moment and then walked to the doorway. "Jackie," I called, "Can you do a couple of letters for me please?"

Jackie followed me back into my office, shorthand notebook and sharpened pencil clutched in her hand. She must have heard all of my end of the telephone conversation but she was far too professional to refer to it. She sat in one of the upright chairs, pencil poised and waited. I took a few moments to try

99

to remember the substance of each of the letters that should have left two days previously.

Ten minutes later, Jackie was back at her desk, typing industriously. Forty minutes after that I was signing each of the letters, with a steaming cup of tea sitting on my desk, which Jackie evidently thought I needed. She was right.

Once again, without the support of a secretary, work piled up and I was still at my desk at seven o'clock that evening when the phone rang.

It was the owner of the secretarial agency.

I picked up the phone but before I could say anything, the lady started speaking. Usually when I had spoken with her she had been polished and unflappable. Now she was clearly upset. "That bloody woman," she began. I thought I detected a sob accompanied by an intake of breath. "That bloody woman," she said again. "She's finished with us. She's foul. She's violent. She threatened me. I should call the police." She continued in much the same vein for several minutes while I listened. At length I said, "well, her previous boss seems vindicated and I think we are both well rid of her."

"Yes," said the agency owner . "Anyway, I thought I should let you know. I'm sorry she was inflicted on you." She paused, then continued "…we haven't got anyone else available who would suit the role," then there was another pause, she seemed to be thinking. Eventually, recovering a bit of composure she said, "there might be one possibility, but I'll have to give it some thought. I'll call you tomorrow.

I bade her goodnight and put the phone down. I leaned back in my chair, feeling relieved and reflecting that I seemed to have had a narrow escape.

100

Next morning the lady from the agency phoned as I was contemplating the pile of assorted envelopes and packages covering my desk while I finished my morning cup of coffee. This was a chore which had devolved upon me ever since the unlamented departure of the lady who had originally occupied the secretarial chair in front of the computer screen. It had been six months now since her role had been declared redundant and although my days were long, I felt that I, as well as the business, were both better off without her. Now however, I was looking forward to the end of opening the morning mail and typing my own letters. Following the disaster of the previous few days I still needed a secretary.

"I've got one possibility, although she doesn't quite fit the profile you were looking for." The voice sounded stressed and hesitant. I could detect that she had not yet recovered from the drama of the evening before.

"Tell me more." I said.

The voice was slightly distorted by the telephone but I detected some easing of the tension. She had probably assumed that following my experience of the hopeless candidate she had put forward, I would be taking my business elsewhere.

I needed a secretary.

"Well, this one is younger, she's keen, has good shorthand and fairly good typing...," she paused and I chipped in.

"Just tell me the downside," I said, "there obviously is one."

"I don't think it should be a big problem," she was rushing on now.

"Tell me," I said.

"It's just that English is not her first language." The announcement came out all in a rush, followed by silence.

"You mean she can't speak English?" My voice rose an octave.

"No, no, no! Of course not!"

"Well, what language does she speak?" I pressed on.

The answer came instantly. "French!"

"French?"

"Yes, French. She has a lovely accent and she's ever so nice."

"What is she like as a Secretary. You told me the last one was nice!"

"Oh, she's nothing like that one – can I send her round?" She had moved imperceptibly from 'wounded and shocked' to articulate sales lady. I shrugged, although from the other end of the phone she couldn't see me.

"O.K." I said, somewhat resignedly, "send her round."

"She won't be able to come until she finishes work tomorrow evening. She could be there by seven thirty. Would that be O.K?"

I had nothing to lose. "Yes, fine," I said. There was nothing more to say so we said our formal farewells, and I went home.

The following evening I waited in my office, fiddling about with odd bits of paperwork and laboriously transcribing a recording of the confusing discussion at the meeting of the General Committee which had taken place a week previously. Outside, the rain hammered down into the pavement and my thoughts were briefly disrupted as the noise of the rain increased to blot out most other sounds. I wasn't sure what time my next candidate would arrive. 'After work' was all I had been told. I wondered if I should drift down for a short interlude with the 'barflies' as the regular drinkers had come to be called. Then I realised that a short interlude would be likely to turn into a longer one. Not only did I have to drive home but breathing powerful alcohol fumes might frighten my appointment away. The best thing was to sit and wait. I wondered what sort of individual I would be meeting, musing that she couldn't possibly be worse than the last one.

At half past seven I decided I had waited long enough. I shoved a few papers into my briefcase, locked the safe and moved towards the door. Then the phone rang. It was Kevin the Senior Receptionist. "There's a young lady here, sir," he said. "Says she has an appointment with you." From the tone of his voice I deduced that he did not approve of the visitor and was not convinced that she had an appointment to see me.

""Bring her over to my office," I said, and I put the phone down, cutting off any possible advice. I walked out to the door of the outer office and waited.

A few minutes later Kevin appeared, followed by my visitor. She was soaking wet and looked pretty miserable. I offered my hand and then ushered her into my office. Kevin lurked expectantly in the doorway.

"Thank you Kevin," I said, and then I shut the door.

I indicated a chair on the other side of my desk and she sank gratefully into it. As she placed her large, over-sized handbag on the floor beside her my attention was caught by a growing wet stain on the carpet around the chair. Water seemed to be running out of her hair and in streams down her face as well as from every fold of her inadequate raincoat. I picked up the phone, called Reception and asked Kevin to send me a towel. While we waited for it to arrive I asked her if she knew what the Club was. She didn't, so I started to tell her, as she mopped her black hair and wet face with a handkerchief. Gradually her appearance became tidier and she sat listening carefully, taking in what I had to say, while fixing me with unblinking brown eyes. I noticed that she had a strong, intelligent face.

I finished the explanation with a short description of the job on offer. There was a knock on the door and the towel arrived. I waited while some of the water was mopped up, noting that the wet patch in the carpet seemed to have expanded.

The interview continued and the young lady began to impress me, as she explained what she had been doing, why she was looking for a job and the skills and qualifications she could bring. She did all this in a mellifluous French accented voice which I found captivating. Before she was halfway through I decided she had got the job – if she wanted it.

Half an hour later I rather formally offered her the job and she accepted. I asked her when she could start and she said "immediately".

So began a successful working partnership. She stayed with me for over fifteen years, developing steadily into a superb diplomat and administrator. Unfortunately, with the passing of the years, the delightful French accent faded.

Thankfully, nothing more was ever heard or seen of Ms Elizabeth.

The Garden Party

Every year, several thousand people are invited to attend a Royal Garden Party held, in England, in the ornate park-like grounds of Buckingham Palace and in Scotland in the gardens of the Palace of HollyroodHouse. Usually, four events are held during July, three at Buckingham Palace and one at HollyroodHouse. Several thousand invitations are issued for each occasion. The recipients are identified and selected through a complex but long-standing system designed to ensure that receipt of an invitation will recognise some achievement or perhaps be seen as a reward for 'good works'. Inevitably there will be those who will be invited not because of what they have done but for who they are. These tend to include members of the diplomatic corps, mayors of small country towns, members of parliament and some celebrities.

In addition to these, a significant number of soldiers, sailors and airmen are invited. At one time these invitations were restricted to officers but now they are entirely egalitarian, so the lawns and pathways of the palace grounds are filled with a mixture of splendid and colourful uniforms, pretty dresses surmounted by extravagant hats, and gentlemen kitted out in immaculate black and grey morning dress coats, frequently accompanied by top-hats. It is, in every sense, a peculiarly British gathering.

There are rules. At one time, only unmarried daughters were allowed to accompany their parents, but now that has been extended to include unmarried sons – in both cases above the age of sixteen years. Also in the past, divorced men and women were banned but this rule had to be eased following a string of divorces within the Royal Family. Intriguingly, the invitations, sent in the name of Her Majesty, are not "invitations" to attend, but "commands" to attend. This has been considered particularly useful by some, to justify the time spent away from work and, more importantly, to obtain official recompense of travelling costs.

One very important rule, frequently quoted, is that "It is Her Majesty's express wish that once an individual has been able to attend a Royal Garden Party, they should not expect to be invited to attend on a subsequent occasion." Inevitably there are a few exceptions to this but they are kept to a minimum.

As part of my duties for the Admiralty Board it fell to me each year to receive five hundred invitations to Royal Garden Parties, to advertise the opportunities within the Naval Service, and then to decide who should merit an invitation. For those still actively serving, names would be sent to me through the command structure, accompanied by recommendations from senior officers explaining the merit and justification of each application. I would receive about eight applications for each available place so it was necessary for me to review all the paperwork and come to a fair and reasonable decision as to who should be favoured. I would try to spread the successful applications among all branches of the Naval Service, including the reserve forces and not forgetting the retired veterans.

On the face of it this task appears relatively easy. But that is before all the lobbying, bullying and cunning that is applied by applicants. As the applications started to roll in my telephone would begin to ring regularly and frequently, senior officers would happen by, ostensibly to pass the time of day with me but actually taking opportunities to ensure that their names had not been forgotten and to apply any 'nudge' that they could think of.

* * * * * * * * * *

I was half listening to the burbling background of my car radio as I crawled through the morning rush hour traffic towards the centre of London. My main concentration was, as always, on the taxis, white vans, fancy cars and buses surrounding me, all competing for the few square yards of road as soon as a space, no matter how small, opened up. And because of this I almost missed the item attached to the end of the eight o'clock news. It had been something about an aircraft carrier and I became momentarily irritated as I realised that I had missed the item.

I need not have worried because the item came up again just as I was manoeuvring my car into an appropriate slot at the end of the line of vehicles on Horseguards Parade. I stopped the car and sat, listening while the engine continued to rumble. It transpired that an aircraft carrier had just left Portsmouth Harbour headed for a six month tour in the Far East. The ship had been given a big send-off with cheering, waving crowds lining the dockside and the harbour-side down as far as the grand old 'Still and West' pub in Old Portsmouth. However the big ship had barely cleared the harbour entrance when she came to a grinding, noisy stop, apparently brought about by a catastrophic failure of the main engine gearing system. Within the hour, she had re-entered the harbour rather ignominiously being towed by a big tug, with another smaller one chugging along behind.

Sabotage was suspected and this eventually proved to be the case. A disaffected lovelorn sailor had managed to put sand into the main gearing lubrication system. Of course this piece of information didn't emerge for several months and all I knew as I locked my car and strolled towards the archway leading into Whitehall, was that something had gone wrong, rather embarrassingly, I thought, with one of the Royal Navy's more important ships. I put the matter from my mind as I responded to the noisy salutes of the dismounted cavalrymen guarding the archway.

Later that afternoon, the subject of the injured aircraft carrier popped up again, this time in the form of a signal, delivered to my office by a Ministry Messenger. The signal form was sealed inside a yellow envelope. I slit open the envelope with my unusual paper knife made in the shape of a Malay 'Kriss', pulled out the single sheet of paper and spread it flat on my desk. I read it, and then read it again rather more slowly. The signal was a message from the Commanding Officer of the aircraft carrier whose problem I had been listening to that morning.

I pushed the flimsy paper across to the desk of my assistant, Philip. He read it and looked up, puzzled.

"What do you think of that?" I said.

"Amazing!" He replied, "I'm surprised he's got the time for that, with his broken ship and all."

I picked up the signal and read it again. What it said was that since the ship would not now be leaving for the Far East for some time, the Commanding Officer would be available to attend a Royal Garden Party and he was expecting to receive his invitation. It was one of the most self -serving and arrogant statements I had seen.

Philip handed me a mug of coffee as I drew a sheet of paper towards me and began to draft a reply. I crossed out the first attempt and tried again.

108

I wrote 'Regret that all invitations for this season's Royal Garden Parties now issued. Unable to meet your request.' Philip folded the paper and slipped it into an envelope before disappearing down the corridor in the direction of the Messenger's Office.

I thought that would be the end of the matter. But it wasn't! A couple of hours later the same messenger appeared at my door and handed over another envelope. This response seemed to me even more outrageous than the first one. I can't remember the exact wording but in general the message repeated the original request only this time demanding two invitations, to include the officer's wife, and went on to say that the Queen would be expecting him to attend. It concluded by stating that a failure to receive an invitation would be 'deeply damaging' to the morale of the ship's company. I remarked that the sudden deferment of an attractive cruise to foreign parts might also have a detrimental impact on morale.

Philip said "Just imagine a couple of sailors scrubbing the decks and saying "Cor' innit a bloody shame that the skipper ain't got no invite to the palace."

I gave a wry grin as I drafted a second signal which simply confirmed that there were no spare invitations available. We packed up the office, locked the door and went home. I assumed the Garden Party matter was closed.

* * * * * * * * * *

Next morning, as I returned from the morning conference in the First Sea Lord's office, I heard my phone ringing before I came through the door. Philip had answered it and he passed me the handset as I eased myself behind my desk. I dumped my notes on the desk and took the phone.

"Hello sir. This is Lieutenant Charlie Coles. I'm the Captain's Secretary of HMS... "

I interrupted. "Is this about garden parties?" I demanded.

"Well, yes sir. The thing is, now that there's time it really is important for the Captain to attend a garden party. He wants to go on...

Exasperated, I interrupted again. "Look," I said "I don't have an inexhaustible supply of invitations to the Queen's social events. I get a limited allocation, which is always over-subscribed, and they have all been distributed. I am not in a position to demand more from the palace and I am certainly not going to withdraw any that have been already sent out. Can you please give my compliments to your Captain and tell him that. Goodbye." I put the phone down.

An hour later, the phone rang again. This time it was the Executive Officer of the damaged aircraft carrier. He started to pass the same message, trying to make it a little more forceful. I waited while the demands and pleas churned on. He spent several minutes expounding the devastation which would be inflicted on his ship's company when they realised that their leader would be unable to enjoy afternoon tea in the presence of Her Majesty. He also managed to weave a threatening tone into his diatribe, suggesting darkly that complaints would be made about my intransigence. Clearly he had absolutely no idea of my relationship with the Members of the Admiralty Board.

When he finished, I spoke slowly and carefully into the 'phone. "I have already said," I explained, "that there is a set and limited number of Royal invitations and they have all been issued. I understand how upset your boss may be and you can tell him that I will of course explain his concerns to the Second Sea Lord when I go to see him in a moment. If he decides to

give up his own invitation, I will let you know." I finished by saying, "oh dear, I must go now, the First Sea Lord wants to speak to me. Something about Boards of Enquiry I believe." I left that barb hanging in the ether as I gently replaced the handset.

That was the last plea that I heard on behalf of the unfortunate aircraft carrier captain, but my garden party problems were not yet over. Later on that afternoon, the scowling, craggy face of a self-proclaimed Very Important Person peered around my partially opened door. I recognised the arrival of more trouble as I climbed slowly to my feet.

"eh, Good afternoon. I was wondering when my wife and I might receive our invitations to the Palace?" The face twisted itself into a frightening shape, with open mouth and prominent discoloured teeth, no doubt what its owner considered to be an engaging smile. This Surgeon Rear Admiral was a serial problem as far as Royal invitations were concerned. He expected to be included, with his wife and daughters, to at least one Royal Garden Party every year, grandly ignoring the views of the Monarch in this regard.

"I think all of the invitations will have been sent by now, sir," I responded defensively. "It is the Palace that send them out you know." I was still struggling for an escape route, but not very effectively.

"Wh'ell," he drawled, lapsing into his Aberdonian accent, "ye better get onto th' Palace and see that I get one." With that the face disappeared and he was gone.

"He'll be back," I said as the sound of squeaky shoe-leather faded away down the corridor.

I was right. The horrible old goat returned to pester me every other day for the next few weeks and then every day as the garden party dates drew closer. I was determined not to

111

give in but I was also beginning to wilt under his blackmailing onslaught. But then fate intervened. My weekly copy of the London Gazette arrived and Philip was poring through it, searching for announcements of promotions or awards which should interest my domain.

"This is interesting," he called from the other side of the room. The Surgeon Rear Admiral has been appointed Honorary Physician to the Queen. I looked up, immediately sensing a way out of the daily grilling.

"Splendid!" I cried.

Philip looked puzzled.

"As an 'honorary' he can go to a garden party in his own right without having to bother me." What I did not say was that the Royal Household was intensely pragmatic about such things and those grand individuals with 'honorary' appointments were expected to attend such events as working hosts, not as guests. I lost no time in getting on to the Garden Parties Office and arranging for a late invitation to be sent out, and then had a short note sent along to the Surgeon Rear Admiral's office, congratulating him warmly on his Royal appointment and informing him that an open invitation was on its way to him in the post. This meant he would be able to choose which Royal Garden Party he would like to attend. I harboured a thought that the greedy old sod would probably try and attend all three.

I received another visit later that afternoon, complete, this time, with the horrible toothy rictus grin, indicating that the ongoing problem was now regarded as resolved.

* * * * * * * * *

The weeks moved on into high summer without any more of the wheedling, demanding afternoon visits. The three garden parties came and went and I turned my attention to other things. It was with some surprise therefore, when I realised one afternoon that I was being rapidly overtaken by squeaky shoes pounding along behind me, as I was strolling back from one of the Ministerial offices.

"I say," called the detested voice from a few paces behind me. I stopped and turned, pasting an insincere smile on my face as I did so.

"You remember my garden party ticket," he said. I took a step back, recoiling from a mixture of lunch flavoured garlic and cigarette smoke.

"Oh, yes," I said, "I hope you had an enjoyable afternoon."

"I did not." He said standing, feet apart in the exact centre of the corridor, in case I was going to make a run for it. "Do you know what happened?"

I confirmed that I did not know what had happened when he had attended a Royal Garden Party.

"I attended in my capacity of "Queen's Honorary Physician" he said.

"Ah yes, quite so," I said.

He glared at me, looking grim. "They gave me a Red Cross arm band and put me in the First Aid Tent. I didn't even get a cup of tea. Outrageous!" He spluttered his outrage towards me but I was far enough away to avoid the flying spittle.

"Yes, I thought they might do that. But I expect the Queen was pleased." Without giving him a chance to reply I turned and walked away. I could hear his heavy breathing as he remained standing in the corridor. I didn't turn to check whether smoke or fire was actually coming out of his nostrils.

Trooping the Colour

The annual ceremony of Trooping the Colour was about to take place on Horseguard's Parade. Teams of workmen had spent the last week erecting viewing stands on three sides of the parade ground. In the early hours of each weekday morning companies of guardsmen, dressed incongruously in khaki working dress uniforms surmounted by splendid bearskin helmets would march down Birdcage Walk from Wellington Barracks. For an hour they would be quick-marched and slow-marched up and down the parade ground to the bellowed roars of a dozen or so drill sergeants, each wielding pacing sticks.

A bulky brown paper package had arrived on my desk and the contents were now arranged in four dissimilar piles. The biggest pile was of grey and pink tickets, to be used for seats at the dress rehearsal. The dress rehearsal was actually quite an event in its own right. Everybody would take part in the dress rehearsal other than Her Majesty The Queen, and they would all, dukes, princes, colonels and generals, be wearing the same dress, medals and honours that they would wear one week later, when the parade would be reviewed by The Queen.

The three other, much smaller piles of tickets, all for the parade itself, provided tickets for lesser diplomats and other hangers-on, for others invited to attend in the principal stands, and for some VIPs. In this case, VIPs amounted to the admirals who comprised the Admiralty Board, the senior Royal Marine Generals and one or two other senior admirals. It was fair to say that anyone below the rank of Vice-Admiral or Lieutenant General Royal Marines would not get a look-in.

114

These fine gentlemen, there were no ladies with sufficient seniority, would all be seated in the principal stand, just behind the reviewing platform where Her Majesty would stand to take the salute of her guards. They would all be indistinguishable from each other because tradition dictated that they would all be wearing black morning dress.

This was where my problem began. There were just four admirals who were full members of the Admiralty Board. As usual I sent round my note reminding each of them, or rather each of their secretaries, of their invitations to the VIP stand and to attend the reception afterwards in the rooms of the Major General London District. The note also reminded the recipients of the dress for the occasion and while not actually saying so, indicted that the invitation to attend was more in the nature of a command.

Unusually, I was invited, a few days later, to have a word with the Chief of Fleet Support, a knighted full admiral who nevertheless saw himself as something of a man of the people.

When I arrived in his small office, he looked up from his desk and announced in forthright terms that it was his intention to attend the 'Trooping' ceremony wearing his naval uniform. "He was not," he said "going to doll himself up in a top hat and look like a ponce."

I attempted to explain that all the other officers seated around him would be wearing morning dress but he was adamant. He was going to wear uniform. As he continued with this assertion I couldn't help thinking of his uniform cap. The cap could best be described as battered. It had long since lost its original shape and looked rather like a bag of lumps and bumps under white cloth cover. Being something of an 'office warrior' he had very few occasions to appear in uniform these days and on the last occasion I had witnessed, the uniform gave the impression of being somewhat crumpled.

The image of the Royal Navy was at risk

I made my way back to my office, eased myself behind the desk and sat for a while to give the matter some thought. Knowing, as I did the convoluted thought processes of some of my senior officers I reached the conclusion that I was rapidly approaching an unwinnable situation. If I ignored the problem and allowed the admiral to become the butt of jokes, which would be probable from some representatives of the British Army who were likely to be present, a degree of opprobrium would inevitably descend on me and that, I thought, would be a bad thing. I had no wish to be branded as the one who had failed to advise and brief my principals properly.

On the other hand, if I continued to try to press my point with the admiral, or maybe with those around him, I would just get his back up and sour our already sometimes difficult relationship.

I continued to sit and think and then, an idea began to dawn on me. I would speak to an expert; an expert with enough weight to impress my reluctant admiral.

I ferretted through my book of interesting and useful telephone numbers and after a couple of false starts I found myself speaking to 'Silver Stick'. This is a shortened version of an ancient title, the full title being 'Silver Stick in Waiting'. 'Silver Stick' is actually the Commander of the Household Division and is usually a Colonel of either of the cavalry regiments, the Royal Dragoon Guards or sometimes the foot-guards.

Within ten minutes I found myself listening to a voice which matched the ancient title. Although he must have been a busy man he listened to everything I had to say with great patience before coming up with an impressive solution to my perceived problem.

"What is the accepted form of dress for a senior officer attending the 'Trooping'?" I asked.

"You see, it's rather like this, old boy," he said, old world charm enfolding every word, "we in the Household would never dream of instructing anyone as to what they should wear, we just feel that one would wish to look one's best in front of the Monarch."

"Quite so," I responded, not being able to think of anything else to say.

There was a long pause and I could almost hear him thinking over the silent telephone line. Eventually he said, rather quietly, "of course, no one in the Guards would be seen dead in anything other than morning dress on such an occasion.

"How do I get that sentiment across to my admiral?" I asked.

"Well, there would be nobody there who could 'take his name'" said Silver Stick, then he added, slowly and thoughtfully, "except Prince Philip, of course."

"I wonder how that might be arranged?"

"One could prime him, I suppose. He wouldn't want to feel let down by the Navy."

An idea was blossoming in my mind and I thanked Silver Stick warmly, telling him how helpful he had been.

"Think nothing of it old chap. Always willing to help. Give me a tinkle if I can do any more. G'bye."

I dragged out the old typewriter, not wishing to trust the newly arrived infernal computer, and began to type a message. I addressed it to the Admiral's Secretary and it went something like this:

117

From: Flag Lt.
To: A/Sec, Sec to CFS.

I have just spoken to Silver Stick in Waiting regarding Saturday's ceremony of Trooping the Colour. He has assured me that dress for senior officers in the presence of HM The Queen, as at Royal Garden Parties, is expected to be black morning dress.

Silver Stick was kind enough to comment on the possibility of HRH Prince Philip taking issue should any British officer decide to attend Her Majesty's Birthday Parade in, say, uniform. (Inappropriately dressed was actually how he put it.)

In view of CFS's stated intention to attend the ceremony in uniform, I thought you should know.

JAH.

I put the note in an 'internal' envelope, sealed it, marked it Urgent and sent it off down the corridor by hand. This, I noted, allowed just under 48 hours before the start of the parade.

I never received any reply or acknowledgement to my note but I did gain enormous satisfaction later that afternoon as I watched the great man's assistant secretary struggling along the corridor burdened with a large hat box, suit covers and other packages – all marked "Moss Bross – Gentlemen's Formal Hire. Miscellaneous

A Visit to the Seychelles

It was a brilliant, warm, sunny morning as the big Helicopter Carrying Cruiser nosed her way slowly between the smaller islands of the Seychelles Group, moving carefully towards the principal shipping berth in the capital, Victoria. Most of the salt and rust stains accrued during the long passage across the Indian Ocean had been removed, anything that could be polished was now gleaming, the barrels of the six-inch main armament were aligned, pointing impressively over the bows and a pair of Sea King helicopters, also polished to a high shine by the application of copious quantities of WD40, adorned the flight deck. All around the deck edges, sailors were lined up dressed immaculately in white uniforms.

As we moved slowly along, just offshore, the air became infused with the familiar smell of tropical vegetation and everyone was looking forward to a few days ashore, enjoying the delights of what the travel agents described as a tropical paradise. Certainly, the balmy airs, the calm turquoise sea, the powder-white sandy beaches almost within reach, the call of sea and land birds and the perfect sub-tropical temperature all served to justify this description.

The visit to this tropical paradise had been arranged in part to provide a few days of welcome relaxation from the long trek across the ocean and the seemingly never ending exercises with various foreign ships, as well as to refuel and re-stock the ship, pick up mail and prepare for another equally long voyage around the Cape of Good Hope and across the South Atlantic to Rio in Brazil. Our visit to the Seychelles was accompanied by the eight frigates, a single nuclear submarine and three

119

support ships that comprised our Deployment Group. We had all been away from Portsmouth for over seven months now and so throughout the flotilla, thoughts were turning increasingly to home. As the flagship we had the only alongside berth and the rest of our consorts were to anchor in the lagoon formed by the island group.

As is often the case on such 'goodwill' visits, the officers of the Flotilla were to host a reception for local big-wigs and worthies. On this occasion there had, been, apparently, a significant level of guidance from the Foreign Office describing the importance of this particular 'flag-showing' visit, which had then gone on to presume to offer advice on how the ships' officers should behave. The admiral's reaction on receipt of the flow of signals was to describe the advice as a "bloody cheek from a bunch of ignorant windbags with nothing better to occupy their time." The rest of the officers, having been rather out of touch while crossing the Pacific and Indian Oceans, were unaware that the newly independent regime in this former colony was becoming increasingly difficult, making false allegations against the former colonial power and, as some said, developing the fine art of biting the hand that had so indulgently fed them for so many years.

All of this became distilled into a series of increasingly exacting briefings which were given to the officer-hosts prior to their attendance under the ornamental awning now covering the flight deck where the party was to take place.

Actually, although everyone was determined to be on their best behaviour it all turned out to be rather unnecessary. It transpired that we were arriving in the beautiful islands at the same time as an increasingly embittered campaign, ostensibly for independence, but in reality to establish which of the extreme socialist parties should be ascendant after

120

independence. It turned out that when full independence was achieved a year later the pattern of a repressive socialist one-party state quickly emerged – with a few assassinations along the way.

At ten minutes to six the officers' of the Flotilla assembled, all immaculately clad in white-jacketed evening dress, complete with miniature medals and 'wings'. Guests began to come aboard, the ship's band started to play gentle background music, and stewards moved forward with trays of champagne, gin and tonic and 'horses necks' (brandy and dry ginger). The party had been going for fifteen minutes and was just warming up when the official delegation arrived. They were dressed in a mixture of fancy uniforms and white dinner jackets and as they came across the gangway onto the flight deck, the admiral, smiling genially, hand outstretched and accompanied by his flag lieutenant moved forward to greet his important guests.

The hand of welcome was ignored and the group of perhaps a dozen men moved across the flight deck, where the admiral, started to introduce some of the senior officers. It was noteworthy that each of the official party collected a chilled glass of champagne as they moved into centre stage. Elsewhere the party seemed to be going well, and more guests were coming over the gangway.

Suddenly, it seemed, all eyes were turned towards a commotion in the middle of the flight deck. The leader of the official party, a tall bearded man with a permanent scowl was now standing with arms spread wide while volubly addressing some sort of complaint towards the admiral, who stood facing the rudeness in shocked silence. The shock and silence seemed to spread like a contagion outward from the knot of people in the centre of the deck.

The disgraceful harangue, for that is what it had become, was brought to a dramatic conclusion. The tall man finished whatever he was saying with a triumphal flourish. He then hurled his half-full champagne glass onto the deck in front of the admiral. The glass shattered, spattering the admiral and a couple of other officers with champagne. Several of the other 'official' guests followed suit, while the remainder greedily guzzled what was left in their glasses before they all turned and stalked down the gangway towards a small fleet of cars which had magically appeared on the jetty.

The whole incident lasted no more than five minutes, by which time a couple of stewards had cleared away the smashed glasses and the champagne. The party started to get back into its rhythm, providing in several instances a new source for exciting and interesting discussion, especially among the expats.

The admiral and his flag lieutenant had disappeared from the reception, no doubt to send an appropriately worded 'Flash' precedence signal to London, describing the clumsily contrived scene which had just taken place. Before he reappeared, word went around among the hosts that no less than twenty-six of our sailors had been arrested ashore and taken to the central jail in Victoria. They were charged, it turned out, with riding bicycles without a license!

Several of the officers present recalled a stall set up on the jetty adjacent to the ship shortly after our arrival, where a couple of locals were enthusiastically hiring out bicycles to sailors as they went ashore. This was presumably part two of the official ill-manners we had all just witnessed.

It took three or four hours more before the British Consul was able to utter sufficient threats to induce a change of heart among the local police. By midnight our men were all back onboard and the party was well and truly over.

In order to limit opportunities for the local politicians to contrive any more nonsense it was decided that men would only be allowed ashore in officially controlled groups for the rest of the visit. In effect this meant beach parties. It also meant that about a million pounds of spending would be denied to the island economy. Evidently the local political smart-alecs hadn't thought about that one!

Next day, Sunday, a plan had been hatched to take about a hundred men to Sainte Anne Island, one of a group of smaller islands about three miles from our berth at Victoria. They were to spend the day swimming, snorkelling, sunbathing, having a 'ban-yan' (picnic) and generally relaxing. A call went out for a suitably qualified seaman officer to lead a crew in one of the ship's forty-five foot workboats and ferry the men out to one of the islands where there was a suitable sandy beach and an absence of local police and politicians. The island was across the main lagoon, about six miles from the ship and just out of sight from the cruiser. I had nothing better to do so I volunteered to run the men out in the morning and bring them back at about four that afternoon.

After breakfast I went up to the bridge to be briefed by the Navigation Officer who gave me a chart, explained that the conditions were likely to be benign, the tide wouldn't change much and I would have a crew of two seamen and one engineer. I tucked the folded chart under my arm, collected a Stornophone portable two-way radio and strolled down to where my boat was waiting, by the midships accommodation ladder. Ten minutes later the boat was loaded with ninety happy young sailors all clutching bags and bundled towels and we were casting off in the direction of 'ban-yan beach.

123

The forty-five foot workboat is a big, tough and sturdy vessel, powered by an effective single diesel engine. It is an open boat, the only protection being a short spray-shield in front of the helmsman.

After half an hour chugging along through glassy calm seas I turned to approach the long white sand beach where I was to discharge my happy cargo. I nosed the big boat in gently towards the beach until the bows grounded in the soft sand. The passengers then hopped off over the bows and over both sides, so that, in less than five minutes I was backing the boat off into deeper water. I stopped for a moment to check that no one had experienced a change of mind then put the helm over and roared off in the direction of the cruiser. Without the weight of our passengers we travelled rather faster and only twenty five minutes later I was back onboard, telling the Duty Lieutenant Commander where I had deposited the men.

I whiled away the afternoon until three-thirty when I went down to man up the boat once more. I experienced a frisson of concern as I noticed that the glassy calm conditions of the morning had been replaced by a light chop, pushed along by a fresh breeze. Thirty minutes later my concern had turned mentally into flashing lights and alarm bells as I turned the boat to approach the long beach on Sainte Anne's Island. I could see my passengers crowded along the shore line but I could also see lines of rolling waves marching powerfully towards the shore where they broke in showers of flying spray. I had a problem.

I couldn't contemplate leaving the men behind but in approaching the beach in those conditions there was a very real risk that I would be leaving the boat as well as the men behind. As I approached the beach the onshore waves were catching the stern of the boat, threatening to turn it sideways on to the beach and end up broached on the sand.

124

I decided to call the ship using the stornophone to ask for advice. However five or six attempts produced no response and so the stornophone was living up to its reputation of being completely unreliable and fairly useless as a means of communication. I was on my own.

I stationed both seamen up in the bows and edged very cautiously through the surf. I made three attempts, backing off rapidly each time to enable me to judge how the boat would behave in the exacting conditions. As I made my fourth cautious run in at ninety degrees to the beach, a column of men formed, wading out through the shallower surf, holding their bundles above their heads. Helped by my men in the bows they began scrambling aboard but only about a dozen made it before the boat started to swing alarmingly to parallel the beach. I rammed the gear lever into reverse and roared off the beach into deep water, took a long breath and began to nose carefully back towards the surf. I got a couple more this time but I was conscious of the waves getting bigger.

I thought of deploying the small kedge anchor on a long line from the stern but in the very soft sand it wouldn't hold, and I was, anyway, unhappy about having a lot of rope out over the stern just where I would need to back off from each run at the beach. I made probably another twenty-five runs into that beach before I backed off for the final time, with everybody aboard.

I was streaming with sweat, exhausted and determined never again to volunteer for such a journey as this, when some comedian stood beside me at the helm, and with a serious face said, Could we go back in one more time sir, I think I left my towel on the beach. My answer, I am afraid, was not printable.

125

Fire on the Road

I was on my way home from RAF Strike Command Headquarters at High Wycombe. The Friday afternoon journey had, as usual been tedious, with crawling traffic on parts of the M3 as well as the roads connecting Reading with Basingstoke. I had now emerged onto the single carriageway roads and with only about 20 miles to run I was looking forward to spending the end of the afternoon in the garden, enjoying the last of the sunshine.

Most of the weekend traffic seemed to have melted away as I cruised towards the roundabout marking the eastern entrance to the small Dorset market town of Wimborne. This particular roundabout rejoices in the strange and unforgettable name of "Canford Bottom" and I was idly contemplating the emergence of such a name as I began to slow down to enter the roundabout. With about a hundred and fifty yards to go my attention was drawn to some sort of commotion taking place on the opposite side of the road, where the east-going road emerges from the roundabout.

A knot of people seemed to be milling around a small white panel van, from the far side of which emerged a column of smoke. The people seemed agitated, running back and forth and waving their arms about. Without really thinking about it I slowed the car further and pulled into a lay-by placed conveniently just beyond the events on the other side of the road.

I climbed out of my car, clicked the key fob to lock the door and strolled nonchalantly across the road to see what was happening. I was still wearing my naval uniform, which seemed to produce the curious effect of causing the small crowd to open up in front of me, falling back as I approached. It was as though they had been expecting me to arrive and quickly solve the problem facing them. As the crowd fell back I saw, with a shock, the cause of the commotion. The column of smoke was actually pouring from the front of a small car, previously invisible behind the bigger panel van. The smoke I had seen was coming from the top of a column of flames, emerging from several parts of the crumpled bonnet. The air around the car was hot and the paintwork at the front was blistering, black and peeling. The car had only two doors and I could see four men sitting inside, none of them moving. The far side of the car seemed to be locked firmly into the side of the van, which was showing signs of scorching from the burning car.

As I cautiously approached the car, a man appeared from the smoke.

"It's jammed," he shouted, "I can't get in."

I assumed he meant the nearside door. Tentatively I reached forward and touched the door handle. It was warm, but mercifully, not too hot to hold. I grabbed it with both hands and heaved. Nothing happened. My anonymous companion stepped forward once more and wrenched at the door handle but also with no result.

I tried again. The door didn't move but I thought I could hear a metallic noise – a very brief grating sound. The flames were getting taller and smoke was by now streaming into the interior of the car from the dashboard which was clearly on fire on its other side, with small flames licking around the edges and probing through the instruments. The men inside the car remained immobile despite the efforts of two women who were hammering on the side window behind the door.

I tried again, grabbing the door handle and subconsciously noting that it had become much hotter. I stepped back and kicked the door as hard as I could. Then I grabbed the handle again, bracing my right foot against the door and gave a mighty heave, throwing all of my body weight into it. The door moved! I heaved again and the door groaned and creaked slowly open about six inches. My companion got both hands onto the edge of the door and together we pulled at it. It resisted stubbornly for a few seconds before suddenly springing open and dumping me on my back on the grass verge.

I scrambled forward on my knees as quickly as I could. A seat belt lock appeared right in front of my face so I unclipped it and, still on my knees, pulled the occupant sideways onto the grass. He fell out of the car and lay, unmoving, beside it. Hands appeared from somewhere and dragged him away.

From my position at the, now open, front door I could see the other three men sitting upright in the car, surrounded by thickening tendrils of smoke. Time was obviously running out so I plunged forward across the front passenger seat and found the seat belt buckle of the driver. It was easy to release and I started to drag the flopping body across the gear lever, handbrake and passenger seat. There was no room for anyone else to get through the single open door so it was up to me. It seemed to take ages but was probably less than a minute before he rolled out to lie unmoving, in the same spot occupied by his companion only a few moments previously. Again people came to drag him away.

My exertions of the past few minutes seemed to have produced a surge of adrenaline within me and I turned to tackle the rear seat passengers who were still not moving, surrounded by thickening smoke and in a desperate state.

128

I tilted the front seat forward but there was insufficient room for me to reach the first man in the back of the car. I fumbled around the front of the seat and eventually found the catch controlling the seat adjustment slide. I wrenched the folded seat forward but there was still not enough room.

I really don't know what happened next but after launching myself in a frenetic attack on the folded front seat, heaving and jerking at it, I suddenly found that I was holding it in my arms, completely detached from the rest of the car.

The dashboard of the car was now well alight and generating a lot of smoke which was causing me to gag and choke. I launched myself into the back of the car and struggled to drag the rather larger man forward and eventually to tumble him onto the grass. Without waiting, I dived into the back of the car again, by now unable to see through the smoke filling the vehicle. I found the seat buckle by touch, released it and started to drag the inert body forwards, as I struggled, crouching, backwards. Eventually he was out and lying on the grass. I squatted beside the open car door and glanced backward to where people were working enthusiastically on the four men now lying supine on the wide grass verge.

The heat emerging from the burning interior of the car was now becoming very uncomfortable as I started to climb to my feet. Almost immediately somebody else appeared beside me and thrust a small fire extinguisher into my hand. I wondered for a moment why he hadn't used his fire extinguisher himself. At the same time I switched on the fire extinguisher and aimed it at the flaming, melted mess that had been the dashboard and instruments. After a minute or so I seemed to be winning, having driven the flames, if not the smoke, back beyond the car interior. At that point the fire extinguisher ran out of puff and failed. With a great whoosh, seemingly delighted and

129

triumphal, the flames surged, full bore, back into the car. I kept the dead extinguisher in my hand as I threw myself to the left and out of the car.

As I picked myself up I saw that the white van was also now well alight and both vehicles were shrouded in smoke from which flames emerged at various points around and above the bonfire. The road was completely blocked by a wall of thick smoke and I asked one of the men standing within the group surrounding the four young men lying on the grass to see if he could get to the other side of the smoke wall and prevent any traffic from trying to drive through it. At this moment a slight figure wearing a suit of overalls stumbled out of the smoke. It was the van driver, who I remembered guiltily, had last been seen staggering about in the middle of the road in a state of dazed shock. He had no idea of what had happened, or where, what or who he was. He was taken by the arm and led back away from the fire to sit on the grass beside the four young men, some of whom were at last beginning to stir.

The flow of traffic coming towards Wimborne from the other side of the fire had stopped and the smoke was swirling and drifting in the light wind, to form an apparently solid dark grey wall across the road. Suddenly, a motorcycle came roaring through the smoke with the front wheel held high in the classic "wheelie" position. The young fool dropped the front wheel back onto the road as he came out of the smoke and roared off towards Wimborne, leaning hard over as he hurtled around the roundabout.

As the 'brain-dead' motorcyclist disappeared from view the fire seemed to find extra energy and the flames were now flowing over, around and under both vehicles. I expected something dramatic as the car's petrol tank was engulfed and I was not disappointed. With a rumble followed by a roar, a jet

130

of flame shot vertically upward from the rear of the car, reaching colourfully to a height of about thirty feet. A few seconds later the first fire engine arrived. I attempted to brief the lead fireman – appropriate, I thought since I had inadvertently become the man in charge of the rescue and the subsequent situation. The fireman simply ignored me so I stood back and waited until a police car drifted up and the occupant strolled towards where the fire was now coming under control. I walked over to him, gave him my name and address and told him what I had seen and done. He seemed nearly as disinterested as the fireman but he did make a few notes in his notebook.

Finally, a couple of ambulances arrived and I stood around while the four survivors that I had pulled from the burning car were loaded into the ambulances. They were all evidently alive but still very much in a state of shock, as was the van driver who was helped to walk into one of the ambulances. They all seemed very young, lying on their stretchers and I thought that they were probably sailors, heading home from Portland or Plymouth for a long weekend.

The situation seemed to be in hand and there didn't seem to be anything more for me to do so I strolled across the road to my ash-covered car, climbed in and drove home. My face was blackened with soot, my hair was slightly singed and my clothing stank of smoke.

When my wife asked me what had caused me to look like a part-time guy-fawkes I said, as I sipped my iced Pimms, "oh, nothing unusual; just routine stuff. I pulled over temporarily to save four young lads trapped in a burning car, and then I came on home.

"What again?" she said referring to another incident which had occurred just one week previously. That one had not been so dramatic, as I had come across a car parked in a lay-by with the engine on fire and the unfortunate lady driver standing beside it. I put out the fire quite quickly, using my own extinguisher and then waited until the AA turned up.

"Oh," said my wife, looking keenly at my dishevelled state "did anyone say thank-you."

"No," I replied, taking another sip of the Pimms , while watching the goldfish competing for their supper in the pond.

"Oh." Was all she said.

In fact no one ever did thank me, either at the time or later. I have often wondered who those four young men were, and whether they ever gave a thought to who had been responsible for saving their lives that sunny afternoon in Dorset.

The End